THE Jungle Books VOL 2

"DARZEE, THE TAILOR-BIRD, IN THE NEST" (*page* 7)

THE Jungle Books

by RUDYARD KIPLING

with illustrations by Aldren Watson

VOLUME TWO

Doubleday & Company, Inc
GARDEN CITY   NEW YORK

DESIGNED BY OSCAR OGG

CONTENTS

VOLUME TWO

COLOR ILLUSTRATIONS

"RIKKI-TIKKI-TAVI"

"RIKKI-TIKKI-TAVI"

At the hole where he went in
Red-Eye called to Wrinkle-Skin.
Hear what little Red-Eye saith:
"Nag, come up and dance with death!"

Eye to eye and head to head,
    (Keep the measure, Nag.)
This shall end when one is dead;
    (At thy pleasure, Nag.)
Turn for turn and twist for twist—
    (Run and hide thee, Nag.)
Hah! The hooded Death has missed!
    (Woe betide thee, Nag!)

THIS IS the story of the great war that Rikki-tikki-tavi fought single-handed, through the bath-rooms of the big bungalow in Segowlee cantonment. Darzee, the tailor-bird, helped him, and Chuchundra, the musk-rat, who never comes out into the middle of the floor, but always creeps round by the wall, gave him advice; but Rikki-tikki did the real fighting.

He was a mongoose, rather like a little cat in his fur and his tail, but quite like a weasel in his head and his habits. His eyes and the end of his restless nose were pink; he could scratch himself anywhere he pleased, with any leg, front or back, that he chose to use; he could fluff up his tail till it looked like a bottle-brush, and his war-cry, as he scuttled through the long grass, was: *"Rikk-tikk-tikki-tikki-tchk!"*

One day, a high summer flood washed him out of the burrow where he lived with his father and mother, and carried him, kicking and clucking, down a roadside ditch. He found a little wisp of grass floating there, and clung to it till he lost his senses. When he revived, he was lying in the hot sun on the middle of a garden path, very draggled indeed, and a small boy was saying: "Here's a dead mongoose. Let's have a funeral."

"No," said his mother; "let's take him in and dry him. Perhaps he isn't really dead."

They took him into the house, and a big man picked him up between his finger and thumb, and said he was not dead but half choked; so they wrapped him in cotton-wool, and warmed him, and he opened his eyes and sneezed.

"Now," said the big man (he was an Englishman who had just moved into the bungalow); "don't frighten him, and we'll see what he'll do."

It is the hardest thing in the world to frighten a mongoose, because he is eaten up from nose to tail with curiosity. The motto of all the mongoose family is, "Run and find out"; and Rikki-tikki was a true mongoose. He looked at the cotton-wool, decided that it was not good to eat, ran all round the table, sat up and put his fur in order, scratched himself, and jumped on the small boy's shoulder.

"Don't be frightened, Teddy," said his father. "That's his way of making friends."

"Ouch! He's tickling under my chin," said Teddy. Rikki-tikki looked down between the boy's collar and neck, snuffed at his ear, and climbed down to the floor, where he sat rubbing his nose.

"Good gracious," said Teddy's mother, "and that's a wild creature! I suppose he's so tame because we've been kind to him."

"All mongooses are like that," said her husband. "If Teddy doesn't pick him up by the tail, or try to put him in a cage, he'll run in and out of the house all day long. Let's give him something to eat."

They gave him a little piece of raw meat. Rikki-tikki liked it immensely, and when it was finished he went out into the verandah and sat in the sunshine and fluffed up his fur to make it dry to the roots. Then he felt better.

"There are more things to find out about in this house," he said to himself, "than all my family could find out in all their lives. I shall certainly stay and find out."

He spent all that day roaming over the house. He nearly drowned himself in the bath-tubs, put his nose into the ink on a writing table, and burnt it on the end of the big man's cigar, for he climbed up in the big

man's lap to see how writing was done. At nightfall he
ran into Teddy's nursery to watch how kerosene-
lamps were lighted, and when Teddy went to bed
Rikki-tikki climbed up too; but he was a restless com-
panion, because he had to get up and attend to every
noise all through the night, and find out what made it.
Teddy's mother and father came in, the last thing, to
look at their boy, and Rikki-tikki was awake on the
pillow. "I don't like that," said Teddy's mother; "he
may bite the child." "He'll do no such thing," said the
father. "Teddy's safer with that little beast than if he
had a bloodhound to watch him. If a snake came into
the nursery now——"

But Teddy's mother wouldn't think of anything so
awful.

Early in the morning Rikki-tikki came to early
breakfast in the verandah riding on Teddy's shoulder,
and they gave him banana and some boiled egg; and he
sat on all their laps one after the other, because every
well-brought-up mongoose always hopes to be a house-
mongoose some day and have rooms to run about in,
and Rikki-tikki's mother (she used to live in the General's house at Segowlee) had carefully told Rikki
what to do if ever he came across white men.

Then Rikki-tikki went out into the garden to see
what was to be seen. It was a large garden, only half
cultivated, with bushes as big as summer-houses of
Marshal Niel roses, lime and orange trees, clumps of
bamboos, and thickets of high grass. Rikki-tikki licked
his lips. "This is a splendid hunting-ground," he said,
and his tail grew bottle-brushy at the thought of it,
and he scuttled up and down the garden, snuffing here
and there till he heard very sorrowful voices in a
thorn-bush.

It was Darzee, the tailor-bird, and his wife. They

had made a beautiful nest by pulling two big leaves together and stitching them up the edges with fibres, and had filled the hollow with cotton and downy fluff. The nest swayed to and fro, as they sat on the rim and cried.

"What is the matter?" asked Rikki-tikki.

"We are very miserable," said Darzee. "One of our babies fell out of the nest yesterday, and Nag ate him."

"H'm!" said Rikki-tikki, "that is very sad—but I am a stranger here. Who is Nag?"

Darzee and his wife only cowered down in the nest without answering, for from the thick grass at the foot of the bush there came a low hiss—a horrid cold sound that made Rikki-tikki jump back two clear feet. Then inch by inch out of the grass rose up the head and spread hood of Nag, the big black cobra, and he was five feet long from tongue to tail. When he had lifted one-third of himself clear of the ground, he stayed balancing to and fro exactly as a dandelion-tuft balances in the wind, and he looked at Rikki-tikki with the wicked snake's eyes that never change their expression, whatever the snake may be thinking of.

"Who is Nag?" said he. "*I* am Nag. The great god Brahm put his mark upon all our people when the first cobra spread his hood to keep the sun off Brahm as he slept. Look, and be afraid!"

He spread out his hood more than ever, and Rikki-tikki saw the spectacle-mark on the back of it that looks exactly like the eye part of a hook-and-eye fastening. He was afraid for the minute; but it is impossible for a mongoose to stay frightened for any length of time, and though Rikki-tikki had never met a live cobra before, his mother had fed him on dead ones, and he knew that all a grown mongoose's business in life was to fight and eat snakes. Nag knew that too, and at the bottom of his cold heart he was afraid.

"Well," said Rikki-tikki, and his tail began to fluff up again, "marks or no marks, do you think it is right for you to eat fledglings out of a nest?"

Nag was thinking to himself, and watching the least little movement in the grass behind Rikki-tikki. He knew that mongooses in the garden meant death sooner or later for him and his family, but he wanted to get Rikki-tikki off his guard. So he dropped his head a little, and put it on one side.

"Let us talk," he said. "You eat eggs. Why should not I eat birds?"

"Behind you! Look behind you!" sang Darzee.

Rikki-tikki knew better than to waste time in staring. He jumped up in the air as high as he could go, and just under him whizzed by the head of Nagaina, Nag's wicked wife. She had crept up behind him as he was talking, to make an end of him; and he heard her savage hiss as the stroke missed. He came down almost across her back, and if he had been an old mongoose he would have known that then was the time to break her back with one bite; but he was afraid of the terrible lashing return-stroke of the cobra. He bit, indeed, but did not bite long enough, and he jumped clear of the whisking tail, leaving Nagaina torn and angry.

"Wicked, wicked Darzee!" said Nag, lashing up as high as he could reach toward the nest in the thornbush; but Darzee had built it out of reach of snakes, and it only swayed to and fro.

Rikki-tikki felt his eyes growing red and hot (when a mongoose's eyes grow red, he is angry), and he sat back on his tail and hind legs like a little kangaroo, and looked all round him, and chattered with rage. But Nag and Nagaina had disappeared into the grass.

When a snake misses its stroke, it never says anything or gives any sign of what it means to do next. Rikki-tikki did not care to follow them, for he did not feel sure that he could manage two snakes at once. So he trotted off to the gravel path near the house, and sat down to think. It was a serious matter for him.

If you read the old books of natural history, you will find they say that when the mongoose fights the snake and happens to get bitten, he runs off and eats some herb that cures him. That is not true. The victory is only a matter of quickness of eye and quickness of foot,—snake's blow against mongoose's jump,—and as no eye can follow the motion of a snake's head when it strikes, that makes things much more wonderful than any magic herb. Rikki-tikki knew he was a young mongoose, and it made him all the more pleased to think that he had managed to escape a blow from behind. It gave him confidence in himself, and when Teddy came running down the path, Rikki-tikki was ready to be petted.

But just as Teddy was stooping, something flinched a little in the dust, and a tiny voice said: "Be careful. I am death!" It was Karait, the dusty brown snakeling that lies for choice on the dusty earth; and his bite is as dangerous as the cobra's. But he is so small that nobody thinks of him, and so he does the more harm to people.

Rikki-tikki's eyes grew red again, and he danced up to Karait with the peculiar rocking, swaying motion that he had inherited from his family. It looks very funny, but it is so perfectly balanced a gait that you can fly off from it at any angle you please; and in dealing with snakes this is an advantage. If Rikki-tikki had only known, he was doing a much more dangerous thing than fighting Nag, for Karait is so small, and

can turn so quickly, that unless Rikki bit him close
to the back of the head, he would get the return-
stroke in his eye or lip. But Rikki did not know: his
eyes were all red, and he rocked back and forth, looking for a good place to hold. Karait struck out. Rikki
jumped sideways and tried to run in, but the wicked
little dusty gray head lashed within a fraction of his
shoulder, and he had to jump over the body, and the
head followed his heels close.

Teddy shouted to the house: "Oh, look here! Our
mongoose is killing a snake"; and Rikki-tikki heard a
scream from Teddy's mother. His father ran out with
a stick, but by the time he came up, Karait had lunged
out once too far, and Rikki-tikki had sprung, jumped
on the snake's back, dropped his head far between his
fore-legs, bitten as high up the back as he could get
hold, and rolled away. That bite paralysed Karait, and
Rikki-tikki was just going to eat him up from the tail,
after the custom of his family at dinner, when he remembered that a full meal makes a slow mongoose,
and if he wanted all his strength and quickness ready,
he must keep himself thin.

He went away for a dust-bath under the castor-oil
bushes, while Teddy's father beat the dead Karait.
"What is the use of that?" thought Rikki-tikki. "I
have settled it all"; and then Teddy's mother picked
him up from the dust and hugged him, crying that he
had saved Teddy from death, and Teddy's father said
that he was a providence, and Teddy looked on with
big scared eyes. Rikki-tikki was rather amused at all
the fuss, which, of course, he did not understand.
Teddy's mother might just as well have petted Teddy
for playing in the dust. Rikki was thoroughly enjoy-
ing himself.

That night, at dinner, walking to and fro among the

wine-glasses on the table, he could have stuffed him-self three times over with nice things; but he remem-bered Nag and Nagaina, and though it was very pleas-ant to be patted and petted by Teddy's mother, and to sit on Teddy's shoulder, his eyes would get red from time to time, and he would go off into his long war-cry of *"Rikk-tikk-tikki-tikki-tchk!"*

Teddy carried him off to bed, and insisted on Rikki-tikki sleeping under his chin. Rikki-tikki was too well bred to bite or scratch, but as soon as Teddy was asleep he went off for his nightly walk round the house, and in the dark he ran up against Chuchundra, the musk-rat, creeping round by the wall. Chuchundra is a broken-hearted little beast. He whimpers and cheeps all the night, trying to make up his mind to run into the middle of the room, but he never gets there.

"Don't kill me," said Chuchundra, almost weeping. "Rikki-tikki, don't kill me."

"Do you think a snake-killer kills musk-rats?" said Rikki-tikki scornfully.

"Those who kill snakes get killed by snakes," said Chuchundra, more sorrowfully than ever. "And how am I to be sure that Nag won't mistake me for you some dark night?"

"There's not the least danger," said Rikki-tikki; "but Nag is in the garden, and I know you don't go there."

"My cousin Chua, the rat, told me——" said Chu-chundra, and then he stopped.

"Told you what?"

"H'sh! Nag is everywhere, Rikki-tikki. You should have talked to Chua in the garden."

"I didn't—so you must tell me. Quick, Chuchundra, or I'll bite you!"

Chuchundra sat down and cried till the tears rolled

off his whiskers. "I am a very poor man," he sobbed. "I never had spirit enough to run out into the middle of the room. H'sh! I mustn't tell you anything. Can't you *hear*, Rikki-tikki?"

Rikki-tikki listened. The house was as still as still, but he thought he could just catch the faintest *scratch-scratch* in the world,—a noise as faint as that of a wasp walking on a window-pane,—the dry scratch of a snake's scales on brick-work.

"That's Nag or Nagaina," he said to himself; "and he is crawling into the bath-room sluice. You're right, Chuchundra; I should have talked to Chua."

He stole off to Teddy's bath-room, but there was nothing there, and then to Teddy's mother's bath-room. At the bottom of the smooth plaster wall there was a brick pulled out to make a sluice for the bath-water, and as Rikki-tikki stole in by the masonry curb where the bath is put, he heard Nag and Nagaina whispering together outside in the moonlight.

"When the house is emptied of people," said Nagaina to her husband, "*he* will have to go away, and then the garden will be our own again. Go in quietly, and remember that the big man who killed Karait is the first one to bite. Then come out and tell me, and we will hunt for Rikki-tikki together."

"But are you sure that there is anything to be gained by killing the people?" said Nag.

"Everything. When there were no people in the bungalow, did we have any mongoose in the garden? So long as the bungalow is empty, we are king and queen of the garden; and remember that as soon as our eggs in the melon-bed hatch (as they may to-morrow), our children will need room and quiet."

"I had not thought of that," said Nag. "I will go, but there is no need that we should hunt for Rikki-tikki afterward. I will kill the big man and his wife, and the child if I can, and come away quietly. Then the bungalow will be empty, and Rikki-tikki will go."

Rikki-tikki tingled all over with rage and hatred at this, and then Nag's head came through the sluice, and his five feet of cold body followed it. Angry as he was, Rikki-tikki was very frightened as he saw the size of the big cobra. Nag coiled himself up, raised his head, and looked into the bath-room in the dark, and Rikki could see his eyes glitter.

"Now, if I kill him here, Nagaina will know; and if I fight him on the open floor, the odds are in his favour. What am I to do?" said Rikki-tikki-tavi.

Nag waved to and fro, and then Rikki-tikki heard him drinking from the biggest water-jar that was used to fill the bath. "That is good," said the snake. "Now, when Karait was killed, the big man had a stick. He may have that stick still, but when he comes in to bathe in the morning he will not have a stick. I shall wait here till he comes. Nagaina—do you hear me?— I shall wait here in the cool till daytime."

There was no answer from outside, so Rikki-tikki knew Nagaina had gone away. Nag coiled himself down, coil by coil, round the bulge at the bottom of the water-jar, and Rikki-tikki stayed still as death. After an hour he began to move, muscle by muscle, toward the jar. Nag was asleep, and Rikki-tikki looked at his big back, wondering which would be the best place for a good hold. "If I don't break his back at the first jump," said Rikki, "he can still fight; and if he fights—O Rikki!" He looked at the thickness of the neck below the hood, but that was too much for him; and a bite near the tail would only make Nag savage.

"It must be the head," he said at last; "the head above the hood; and when I am once there, I must not let go."

Then he jumped. The head was lying a little clear

of the water-jar, under the curve of it; and, as his teeth
met, Rikki braced his back against the bulge of the red
earthenware to hold down the head. This gave him
just one second's purchase, and he made the most of
it. Then he was battered to and fro as a rat is shaken
by a dog—to and fro on the floor, up and down, and
round in great circles; but his eyes were red, and he
held on as the body cart-whipped over the floor, upsetting the tin dipper and the soap-dish and the flesh-
brush, and banged against the tin side of the bath. As
he held he closed his jaws tighter and tighter, for he
made sure he would be banged to death, and, for the
honour of his family, he preferred to be found with
his teeth locked. He was dizzy, aching, and felt shaken
to pieces when something went off like a thunderclap
just behind him; a hot wind knocked him senseless, and
red fire singed his fur. The big man had been wakened
by the noise, and had fired both barrels of a shot-gun
into Nag just behind the hood.

Rikki-tikki held on with his eyes shut, for now he
was quite sure he was dead; but the head did not move,
and the big man picked him up and said: "It's the mongoose again, Alice; the little chap has saved *our* lives
now." Then Teddy's mother came in with a very
white face, and saw what was left of Nag, and Rikki-
tikki dragged himself to Teddy's bedroom and spent
half the rest of the night shaking himself tenderly to
find out whether he really was broken into forty
pieces, as he fancied.

When morning came he was very stiff, but well
pleased with his doings. "Now I have Nagaina to settle
with, and she will be worse than five Nags, and there's
no knowing when the eggs she spoke of will hatch.
Goodness! I must go and see Darzee," he said.

Without waiting for breakfast, Rikki-tikki ran to
the thorn-bush where Darzee was singing a song of

triumph at the top of his voice. The news of Nag's death was all over the garden, for the sweeper had thrown the body on the rubbish-heap.

"Oh, you stupid tuft of feathers!" said Rikki-tikki angrily. "Is this the time to sing?"

"Nag is dead—is dead—is dead!" sang Darzee. "The valiant Rikki-tikki caught him by the head and held fast. The big man brought the bang-stick, and Nag fell in two pieces! He will never eat my babies again."

"All that's true enough; but where's Nagaina?" said Rikki-tikki, looking carefully round him.

"Nagaina came to the bath-room sluice and called for Nag," Darzee went on; "and Nag came out on the end of a stick—the sweeper picked him up on the end of a stick and threw him upon the rubbish-heap. Let us sing about the great, the red-eyed Rikki-tikki!" and Darzee filled his throat and sang.

"If I could get up to your nest, I'd roll all your babies out!" said Rikki-tikki. "You don't know when to do the right thing at the right time. You're safe enough in your nest there, but it's war for me down here. Stop singing a minute, Darzee."

"For the great, the beautiful Rikki-tikki's sake I will stop," said Darzee. "What is it, O Killer of the terrible Nag?"

"Where is Nagaina, for the third time?"

"On the rubbish-heap by the stables, mourning for Nag. Great is Rikki-tikki with the white teeth."

"Bother my white teeth! Have you ever heard where she keeps her eggs?"

"In the melon-bed, on the end nearest the wall, where the sun strikes nearly all day. She hid them there weeks ago."

"And you never thought it worth while to tell me? The end nearest the wall, you said?"

"Rikki-tikki, you are not going to eat her eggs?"

"Not eat exactly; no. Darzee, if you have a grain of sense you will fly off to the stables and pretend that your wing is broken, and let Nagaina chase you away to this bush. I must get to the melon-bed, and if I went there now she'd see me."

Darzee was a feather-brained little fellow who could never hold more than one idea at a time in his head; and just because he knew that Nagaina's children were born in eggs like his own, he didn't think at first that it was fair to kill them. But his wife was a sensible bird, and she knew that cobra's eggs meant young cobras later on; so she flew off from the nest, and left Darzee to keep the babies warm, and continue his song about the death of Nag. Darzee was very like a man in some ways.

She fluttered in front of Nagaina by the rubbish-heap, and cried out, "Oh, my wing is broken! The boy in the house threw a stone at me and broke it." Then she fluttered more desperately than ever.

Nagaina lifted up her head and hissed, "You warned Rikki-tikki when I would have killed him. Indeed and truly, you've chosen a bad place to be lame in." And she moved toward Darzee's wife, slipping along over the dust.

"The boy broke it with a stone!" shrieked Darzee's wife.

"Well! It may be some consolation to you when you're dead to know that I shall settle accounts with the boy. My husband lies on the rubbish-heap this morning, but before night the boy in the house will lie very still. What is the use of running away? I am sure to catch you. Little fool, look at me!"

Darzee's wife knew better than to do *that*, for a bird who looks at a snake's eyes gets so frightened that she cannot move. Darzee's wife fluttered on, piping sorrowfully, and never leaving the ground, and Nagaina quickened her pace.

Rikki-tikki heard them going up the path from the stables, and he raced for the end of the melon-patch near the wall. There, in the warm litter about the melons, very cunningly hidden, he found twenty-five eggs, about the size of a bantam's eggs, but with whitish skin instead of shell.

"I was not a day too soon," he said; for he could see the baby cobras curled up inside the skin, and he knew that the minute they were hatched they could each kill a man or a mongoose. He bit off the tops of the eggs as fast as he could, taking care to crush the young cobras, and turned over the litter from time to time to see whether he had missed any. At last there were only three eggs left, and Rikki-tikki began to chuckle to himself, when he heard Darzee's wife screaming:

"Rikki-tikki, I led Nagaina toward the house, and she has gone into the verandah, and—oh, come quickly —she means killing!"

Rikki-tikki smashed two eggs, and tumbled backward down the melon-bed with the third egg in his mouth, and scuttled to the verandah as hard as he could put foot to the ground. Teddy and his mother and father were there at early breakfast; but Rikki-tikki saw that they were not eating anything. They sat stone-still, and their faces were white. Nagaina was coiled up on the matting by Teddy's chair, within easy striking-distance of Teddy's bare leg, and she was swaying to and fro singing a song of triumph.

"Son of the big man that killed Nag," she hissed, "stay still. I am not ready yet. Wait a little. Keep very still, all you three. If you move I strike, and if you do not move I strike. Oh, foolish people, who killed my Nag!"

Teddy's eyes were fixed on his father, and all his father could do was to whisper, "Sit still, Teddy. You mustn't move. Teddy, keep still."

Then Rikki-tikki came up and cried: "Turn round, Nagaina; turn and fight!"

"All in good time," said she, without moving her eyes. "I will settle my account with *you* presently. Look at your friends, Rikki-tikki. They are still and white; they are afraid. They dare not move, and if you come a step nearer I strike."

"Look at your eggs," said Rikki-tikki, "in the melon-bed near the wall. Go and look, Nagaina."

The big snake turned half round, and saw the egg on the verandah. "Ah-h! Give it to me," she said.

Rikki-tikki put his paws one on each side of the egg, and his eyes were blood-red. "What price for a snake's egg? For a young cobra? For a young king-cobra? For the last—the very last of the brood? The ants are eating all the others down by the melon-bed."

Nagaina spun clear round, forgetting everything for the sake of the one egg; and Rikki-tikki saw Teddy's father shoot out a big hand, catch Teddy by the shoulder, and drag him across the little table with the tea-cups, safe and out of reach of Nagaina.

"Tricked! Tricked! Tricked! *Rikk-tck-tck!*" chuckled Rikki-tikki. "The boy is safe, and it was I—I—I that caught Nag by the hood last night in the bath-room." Then he began to jump up and down, all four feet together, his head close to the floor. "He threw me to and fro, but he could not shake me off. He was dead before the big man blew him in two. I did it. *Rikki-tikki-tck-tck!* Come then, Nagaina. Come and fight with me. You shall not be a widow long."

Nagaina saw that she had lost her chance of killing Teddy, and the egg lay between Rikki-tikki's paws.

"Give me the egg, Rikki-tikki. Give me the last of my eggs, and I will go away and never come back," she said, lowering her hood.

"Yes, you will go away, and you will never come back; for you will go to the rubbish-heap with Nag. Fight, widow! The big man has gone for his gun! Fight!"

Rikki-tikki was bounding all round Nagaina, keeping just out of reach of her stroke, his little eyes like hot coals. Nagaina gathered herself together, and flung out at him. Rikki-tikki jumped up and backward. Again and again and again she struck, and each time her head came with a whack on the matting of the verandah, and she gathered herself together like a watch-spring. Then Rikki-tikki danced in a circle to get behind her, and Nagaina spun round to keep her head to his head, so that the rustle of her tail on the matting sounded like dry leaves blown along by the wind.

He had forgotten the egg. It still lay on the verandah, and Nagaina came nearer and nearer to it, till at last, while Rikki-tikki was drawing breath, she caught it in her mouth, turned to the verandah steps, and flew like an arrow down the path, with Rikki-tikki behind her. When the cobra runs for her life, she goes like a whip-lash flicked across a horse's neck.

Rikki-tikki knew that he must catch her, or all the trouble would begin again. She headed straight for the long grass by the thorn-bush, and as he was running Rikki-tikki heard Darzee still singing his foolish little song of triumph. But Darzee's wife was wiser. She flew off her nest as Nagaina came along, and flapped her wings about Nagaina's head. If Darzee had helped they might have turned her; but Nagaina only lowered her hood and went on. Still, the instant's delay brought

Rikki-tikki up to her, and as she plunged into the rat-hole where she and Nag used to live, his little white teeth were clenched on her tail, and he went down with her—and very few mongooses, however wise and old they may be, care to follow a cobra into its hole. It was dark in the hole; and Rikki-tikki never knew when it might open out and give Nagaina room to turn and strike at him. He held on savagely, and struck out his feet to act as brakes on the dark slope of the hot, moist earth.

Then the grass by the mouth of the hole stopped waving, and Darzee said: "It is all over with Rikki-tikki! We must sing his death song. Valiant Rikki-tikki is dead! For Nagaina will surely kill him under-ground."

So he sang a very mournful song that he made up on the spur of the minute, and just as he got to the most touching part the grass quivered again, and Rikki-tikki, covered with dirt, dragged himself out of the hole leg by leg, licking his whiskers. Darzee stopped with a little shout. Rikki-tikki shook some of the dust out of his fur and sneezed. "It is all over," he said. "The widow will never come out again." And the red ants that live between the grass stems heard him, and began to troop down one after another to see if he had spoken the truth.

Rikki-tikki curled himself up in the grass and slept where he was—slept and slept till it was late in the afternoon, for he had done a hard day's work.

"Now," he said, when he awoke, "I will go back to the house. Tell the Coppersmith, Darzee, and he will tell the garden that Nagaina is dead."

The Coppersmith is a bird who makes a noise exactly like the beating of a little hammer on a copper pot; and the reason he is always making it is because he is the town-crier to every Indian garden, and tells all the news to everybody who cares to listen. As Rikki-tikki went up the path, he heard his "attention" notes like a tiny dinner-gong; and then the steady *"Ding-dong-tock! Nag is dead—dong! Nagaina is dead! Ding-dong-tock!"* That set all the birds in the garden singing, and the frogs croaking; for Nag and Nagaina used to eat frogs as well as little birds.

When Rikki got to the house, Teddy and Teddy's mother (she still looked very white, for she had been fainting) and Teddy's father came out and almost cried over him; and that night he ate all that was given him till he could eat no more, and went to bed on Teddy's shoulder, where Teddy's mother saw him when she came to look late at night.

"He saved our lives and Teddy's life," she said to her husband. "Just think, he saved all our lives!"

Rikki-tikki woke up with a jump, for all the mongooses are light sleepers.

"Oh, it's you," said he. "What are you bothering for? All the cobras are dead; and if they weren't, I'm here."

Rikki-tikki had a right to be proud of himself; but he did not grow too proud, and he kept that garden as a mongoose should keep it, with tooth and jump and spring and bite, till never a cobra dared show its head inside the walls.

DARZEE'S CHAUNT

(Sung in honour of Rikki-tikki-tavi)

Singer and tailor am I—
Doubled the joys that I know—
Proud of my lilt through the sky,
Proud of the house that I sew—
Over and under, so weave I my music—so weave I the
house that I sew.

Sing to your fledglings again,
Mother, oh lift up your head!
Evil that plagued us is slain,
Death in the garden lies dead.
Terror that hid in the roses is impotent—flung on the
dung-hill and dead!

Who hath delivered us, who?
Tell me his nest and his name.
Rikki, the valiant, the true,
Tikki, with eyeballs of flame,
Rik-tikki-tikki, the ivory-fangéd, the hunter with eye-
balls of flame.

Give him the Thanks of the Birds,
Bowing with tail-feathers spread!
Praise him with nightingale-words—
Nay, I will praise him instead.
Hear! I will sing you the praise of the bottle-tailed
Rikki, with eyeballs of red!

(Here Rikki-tikki interrupted, and the rest of the song
is lost.)

THE WHITE SEAL

THE WHITE SEAL

Oh! hush thee, my baby, the night is behind us,
    And black are the waters that sparkled so green.
The moon, o'er the combers, looks downward to find
    us
    At rest in the hollows that rustle between.
Where billow meets billow, there soft be thy pillow;
    Ah, weary wee flipperling, curl at thy ease!
The storm shall not wake thee, nor shark overtake
    thee,
    Asleep in the arms of the slow-swinging seas.
                      Seal Lullaby

ALL THESE things happened several years ago at a place called Novastoshnah, or North East Point, on the Island of St. Paul, away and away in the Bering Sea. Limmershin, the Winter Wren, told me the tale when he was blown on to the rigging of a steamer going to Japan, and I took him down into my cabin and warmed and fed him for a couple of days till he was fit to fly back to St. Paul's again. Limmershin is a very odd little bird, but he knows how to tell the truth.

Nobody comes to Novastoshnah except on business, and the only people who have regular business there are the seals. They come in the summer months by hundreds and hundreds of thousands out of the cold gray sea; for Novastoshnah Beach has the finest accommodation for seals of any place in all the world.

Sea Catch knew that, and every spring would swim from whatever place he happened to be in—would swim like a torpedo-boat straight for Novastoshnah, and spend a month fighting with his companions for a good place on the rocks as close to the sea as possible. Sea Catch was fifteen years old, a huge gray fur-seal with almost a mane on his shoulders, and long, wicked dog-teeth. When he heaved himself up on his front flippers he stood more than four feet clear of the ground, and his weight, if any one had been bold enough to weigh him, was nearly seven hundred pounds. He was scarred all over with the marks of savage fights, but he was always ready for just one fight more. He would put his head on one side, as though he were afraid to look his enemy in the face; then he would shoot it out like lightning, and when the big teeth were firmly fixed on the other seal's neck, the other seal might get away if he could, but Sea Catch would not help him.

Yet Sea Catch never chased a beaten seal, for that was against the Rules of the Beach. He only wanted room by the sea for his nursery; but as there were forty or fifty thousand other seals hunting for the same thing each spring, the whistling, bellowing, roaring, and blowing on the beach were something frightful.

From a little hill called Hutchinson's Hill you could look over three and a half miles of ground covered with fighting seals; and the surf was dotted all over with the heads of seals hurrying to land and begin their share of the fighting. They fought in the breakers, they fought in the sand, and they fought on the smooth-worn basalt rocks of the nurseries; for they were just as stupid and unaccommodating as men. Their wives never came to the island until late in May or early in

June, for they did not care to be torn to pieces; and
the young two-, three-, and four-year-old seals who
had not begun housekeeping went inland about half a
mile through the ranks of the fighters and played about
on the sand-dunes in droves and legions, and rubbed
off every single green thing that grew. They were
called the holluschickie,—the bachelors,—and there
were perhaps two or three hundred thousand of them
at Novastoshnah alone.

Sea Catch had just finished his forty-fifth fight one
spring when Matkah, his soft, sleek, gentle-eyed wife,
came up out of the sea, and he caught her by the scruff
of the neck and dumped her down on his reserva-
tion, saying gruffly: "Late, as usual. Where *have* you
been?"

It was not the fashion for Sea Catch to eat anything
during the four months he stayed on the beaches, and
so his temper was generally bad. Matkah knew better
than to answer back. She looked round and cooed:
"How thoughtful of you! You've taken the old place
again."

"I should think I had," said Sea Catch. "Look at
me!"

He was scratched and bleeding in twenty places;
one eye was almost blind, and his sides were torn to
ribbons.

"Oh, you men, you men!" Matkah said, fanning
herself with her hind flipper. "Why can't you be sensible and settle your places quietly? You look as
though you had been fighting with the Killer Whale."

"I haven't been doing anything *but* fight since the
middle of May. The beach is disgracefully crowded
this season. I've met at least a hundred seals from
Lukannon Beach, house-hunting. Why can't people
stay where they belong?"

"I've often thought we should be much happier if

we hauled out at Otter Island instead of this crowded place," said Matkah.

"Bah! Only the holluschickie go to Otter Island. If we went there they would say we were afraid. We must preserve appearances, my dear."

Sea Catch sunk his head proudly between his fat shoulders and pretended to go to sleep for a few minutes, but all the time he was keeping a sharp look-out for a fight. Now that all the seals and their wives were on the land, you could hear their clamour miles out to sea above the loudest gales. At the lowest counting there were over a million seals on the beach,—old seals, mother seals, tiny babies, and holluschickie, fighting, scuffling, bleating, crawling, and playing together,— going down to the sea and coming up from it in gangs and regiments, lying over every foot of ground as far as the eye could reach, and skirmishing about in brigades through the fog. It is nearly always foggy at Novastoshnah, except when the sun comes out and makes everything look all pearly and rainbow-coloured for a little while.

Kotick, Matkah's baby, was born in the middle of that confusion, and he was all head and shoulders, with pale, watery-blue eyes, as tiny seals must be; but there was something about his coat that made his mother look at him very closely.

"Sea Catch," she said at last, "our baby's going to be white!"

"Empty clam-shells and dry seaweed!" snorted Sea Catch. "There never has been such a thing in the world as a white seal."

"I can't help that," said Matkah; "there's going to be now"; and she sang the low, crooning seal-song that all the mother seals sing to their babies:

You mustn't swim till you're six weeks old,
  Or your head will be sunk by your heels;
And summer gales and Killer Whales
  Are bad for baby seals.

Are bad for baby seals, dear rat,
  As bad as bad can be;
But splash and grow strong,
And you can't be wrong,
  Child of the Open Sea!

Of course the little fellow did not understand the
words at first. He paddled and scrambled about by his
mother's side, and learned to scuffle out of the way
when his father was fighting with another seal, and
the two rolled and roared up and down the slippery
rocks. Matkah used to go to sea to get things to eat,
and the baby was fed only once in two days; but then
he ate all he could, and throve upon it.

The first thing he did was to crawl inland, and there
he met tens of thousands of babies of his own age, and
they played together like puppies, went to sleep on the
clean sand, and played again. The old people in the
nurseries took no notice of them, and the holluschickie
kept to their own grounds, so the babies had a beautiful playtime.

When Matkah came back from her deep-sea fishing
she would go straight to their playground and call as a
sheep calls for a lamb, and wait until she heard Kotick
bleat. Then she would take the straightest of straight
lines in his direction, striking out with her fore flippers
and knocking the youngsters head over heels right and
left. There were always a few hundred mothers hunting for their children through the playgrounds, and
the babies were kept lively; but, as Matkah told

Kotick, "So long as you don't lie in muddy water and get mange, or rub the hard sand into a cut or scratch, and so long as you never go swimming when there is a heavy sea, nothing will hurt you here."

Little seals can no more swim than little children, but they are unhappy till they learn. The first time that Kotick went down to the sea a wave carried him out beyond his depth, and his big head sank and his little hind flippers flew up exactly as his mother had told him in the song, and if the next wave had not thrown him back again he would have drowned.

After that he learned to lie in a beach-pool and let the wash of the waves just cover him and lift him up while he paddled, but he always kept his eye open for big waves that might hurt. He was two weeks learning to use his flippers; and all that while he floundered in and out of the water, and coughed and grunted and crawled up the beach and took cat-naps on the sand, and went back again, until at last he found that he truly belonged to the water.

Then you can imagine the times that he had with his companions, ducking under the rollers; or coming in on top of a comber and landing with a swash and a splutter as the big wave went whirling far up the beach; or standing up on his tail and scratching his head as the old people did; or playing "I'm the King of the Castle" on slippery, weedy rocks that just stuck out of the wash. Now and then he would see a thin fin, like a big shark's fin, drifting along close to shore, and he knew that that was the Killer Whale, the Grampus, who eats young seals when he can get them; and Kotick would head for the beach like an arrow, and the fin would jig off slowly, as if it were looking for nothing at all.

Late in October the seals began to leave St. Paul's

for the deep sea, by families and tribes, and there was
no more fighting over the nurseries, and the holluschickie played anywhere they liked. "Next year," said
Matkah to Kotick, "you will be a holluschickie; but
this year you must learn how to catch fish."

They set out together across the Pacific, and Matkah
showed Kotick how to sleep on his back with his flippers tucked down by his side and his little nose just
out of the water. No cradle is so comfortable as the
long, rocking swell of the Pacific. When Kotick felt
his skin tingle all over, Matkah told him he was learning the "feel of the water," and that tingly, prickly
feelings meant bad weather coming, and he must swim
hard and get away.

"In a little time," she said, "you'll know where to
swim to, but just now we'll follow Sea Pig, the Por-
poise, for he is very wise." A school of porpoises were
ducking and tearing through the water, and little
Kotick followed them as fast as he could. "How do
you know where to go?" he panted. The leader of the
school rolled his white eyes, and ducked under. "My
tail tingles, youngster," he said. "That means there's
a gale behind me. Come along! When you're south of
the Sticky Water [he meant the Equator], and your
tail tingles, that means there's a gale in front of you
and you must head north. Come along! The water
feels bad here."

This was one of the very many things that Kotick
learned, and he was always learning. Matkah taught
him to follow the cod and the halibut along the under-
sea banks, and wrench the rockling out of his hole
among the weeds; how to skirt the wrecks lying a
hundred fathoms below water, and dart like a rifle-
bullet in at one port-hole and out at another as the
fishes ran; how to dance on the top of the waves when

the lightning was racing all over the sky, and wave his flipper politely to the stumpy-tailed Albatross and the Man-of-war Hawk as they went down the wind; how to jump three or four feet clear of the water, like a dolphin, flippers close to the side and tail curved; to leave the flying-fish alone because they are all bony; to take the shoulder-piece out of a cod at full speed ten fathoms deep; and never to stop and look at a boat or a ship, but particularly a row-boat. At the end of six months, what Kotick did not know about deep-sea fishing was not worth the knowing, and all that time he never set flipper on dry ground.

One day, however, as he was lying half asleep in the warm water somewhere off the Island of Juan Fernandez, he felt faint and lazy all over, just as human people do when the spring is in their legs, and he remembered the good firm beaches of Novastoshnah seven thousand miles away, the games his companions played, the smell of the sea-weed, the seal roar, and the fighting. That very minute he turned north, swimming steadily, and as he went on he met scores of his mates, all bound for the same place, and they said: "Greeting, Kotick! This year we are all holluschickie, and we can dance the Fire-dance in the breakers off Lukannon and play on the new grass. But where did you get that coat?"

Kotick's fur was almost pure white now, and though he felt very proud of it, he only said: "Swim quickly! My bones are aching for the land." And so they all came to the beaches where they had been born, and heard the old seals, their fathers, fighting in the rolling mist.

That night Kotick danced the Fire-dance with the yearling seals. The sea is full of fire on summer nights all the way down from Novastoshnah to Lukannon, and each seal leaves a wake like burning oil behind him, and a flaming flash when he jumps, and the waves break in great phosphorescent streaks and swirls. Then they went inland to the holluschickie grounds, and rolled up and down in the new wild wheat, and told stories of what they had done while they had been at sea. They talked about the Pacific as boys would talk about a wood that they had been nutting in, and if any one had understood them, he could have gone away and made such a chart of that ocean as never was. The three- and four-year-old holluschickie romped down from Hutchinson's Hill, crying: "Out of the way, youngsters! The sea is deep, and you don't know all that's in it yet. Wait till you've rounded the Horn. Hi, you yearling, where did you get that white coat?"

"I didn't get it," said Kotick; "it grew." And just as he was going to roll the speaker over, a couple of black-haired men with flat red faces came from behind a sand-dune, and Kotick, who had never seen a man before, coughed and lowered his head. The holluschickie just bundled off a few yards and sat staring

stupidly. The men were no less than Kerick Booterin, the chief of the seal-hunters on the island, and Patalamon, his son. They came from the little village not half a mile from the seal-nurseries, and they were deciding what seals they would drive up to the killing-pens (for the seals were driven just like sheep), to be turned into sealskin jackets later on.

"Ho!" said Patalamon. "Look! There's a white seal!"

Kerick Booterin turned nearly white under his oil and smoke, for he was an Aleut, and Aleuts are not clean people. Then he began to mutter a prayer. "Don't touch him, Patalamon. There has never been a white seal since—since I was born. Perhaps it is old Zaharrof's ghost. He was lost last year in the big gale."

"I'm not going near him," said Patalamon. "He's unlucky. Do you really think he is old Zaharrof come back? I owe him for some gulls' eggs."

"Don't look at him," said Kerick. "Head off that drove of four-year-olds. The men ought to skin two hundred to-day, but it's the beginning of the season, and they are new to the work. A hundred will do. Quick!"

Patalamon rattled a pair of seal's shoulder-bones in front of a herd of holluschickie, and they stopped dead, puffing and blowing. Then he stepped near, and the seals began to move, and Kerick headed them inland, and they never tried to get back to their companions. Hundreds and hundreds of thousands of seals watched them being driven, but they went on playing just the same. Kotick was the only one who asked questions, and none of his companions could tell him anything, except that the men always drove seals in that way for six weeks or two months of every year.

"I am going to follow," he said, and his eyes nearly

popped out of his head as he shuffled along in the wake of the herd.

"The white seal is coming after us," cried Pata-lamon. "That's the first time a seal has ever come to the killing-grounds alone."

"Hsh! Don't look behind you," said Kerick. "It *is* Zaharrof's ghost! I must speak to the priest about this."

The distance to the killing-grounds was only half a mile, but it took an hour to cover, because if the seals went too fast Kerick knew that they would get heated and then their fur would come off in patches when they were skinned. So they went on very slowly, past Sea-Lion's Neck, past Webster House, till they came to the Salt House just beyond the sight of the seals on the beach. Kotick followed, panting and wondering. He thought that he was at the world's end, but the roar of the seal-nurseries behind him sounded as loud as the roar of a train in a tunnel. Then Kerick sat down on the moss and pulled out a heavy pewter watch and let the drove cool off for thirty minutes, and Kotick could hear the fog-dew dripping from the brim of his cap. Then ten or twelve men, each with an iron-bound club three or four feet long, came up, and Kerick pointed out one or two of the drove that were bitten by their companions or were too hot, and the men kicked those aside with their heavy boots made of the skin of a walrus's throat, and then Kerick said: "Let go!" and then the men clubbed the seals on the head as fast as they could.

Ten minutes later little Kotick did not recognise his friends any more, for their skins were ripped off from the nose to the hind flippers—whipped off and thrown down on the ground in a pile.

That was enough for Kotick. He turned and gal-loped (a seal can gallop very swiftly for a short time) back to the sea, his little new moustache bristling with horror. At Sea-Lion's Neck, where the great sea-lions sit on the edge of the surf, he flung himself flipper overhead into the cool water, and rocked there, gasping miserably. "What's here?" said a sea-lion gruffly; for as a rule the sea-lions keep themselves to themselves.

"*Scoochnie! Ochen scoochnie!*" ("I'm lonesome, very lonesome!") said Kotick. "They're killing *all* the holluschickie on *all* the beaches!"

The sea-lion turned his head inshore. "Nonsense!" he said; "your friends are making as much noise as ever. You must have seen old Kerick polishing off a drove. He's done that for thirty years."

"It's horrible," said Kotick, backing water as a wave went over him, and steadying himself with a screw-stroke of his flippers that brought him up all standing within three inches of a jagged edge of rock.

"Well done for a yearling!" said the sea-lion, who could appreciate good swimming. "I suppose it *is* rather awful from your way of looking at it; but if you seals will come here year after year, of course the men get to know of it, and unless you can find an island where no men ever come, you will always be driven."

"Isn't there any such island?" began Kotick.

"I've followed the *poltoos* [the halibut] for twenty years, and I can't say I've found it yet. But look here— you seem to have a fondness for talking to your betters; suppose you go to Walrus Islet and talk to Sea Vitch. He may know something. Don't flounce off like that. It's a six-mile swim, and if I were you I should haul out and take a nap first, little one."

Kotick thought that that was good advice, so he swam round to his own beach, hauled out, and slept for half an hour, twitching all over, as seals will. Then he headed straight for Walrus Islet, a little low sheet of

rocky island almost due northeast from Novastoshnah,
all ledges of rock and gulls' nests, where the walrus
herded by themselves.

He landed close to old Sea Vitch—the big, ugly,
bloated, pimpled, fat-necked, long-tusked walrus of
the North Pacific, who has no manners except when he
is asleep—as he was then, with his hind flippers half in
and half out of the surf.

"Wake up!" barked Kotick, for the gulls were making a great noise.

"Hah! Ho! Hmph! What's that?" said Sea Vitch,
and he struck the next walrus a blow with his tusks
and waked him up, and the next struck the next, and
so on till they were all awake and staring in every
direction but the right one.

"Hi! It's me," said Kotick, bobbing in the surf and
looking like a little white slug.

"Well! May I be —— skinned!" said Sea Vitch, and
they all looked at Kotick as you can fancy a club full
of drowsy old gentlemen would look at a little boy.
Kotick did not care to hear any more about skinning
just then; he had seen enough of it; so he called out:
"Isn't there any place for seals to go where men don't
ever come?"

"Go and find out," said Sea Vitch, shutting his eyes.
"Run away. We're busy here."

Kotick made his dolphin-jump in the air and shouted
as loud as he could: "Clam-eater! Clam-eater!" He
knew that Sea Vitch never caught a fish in his life, but
always rooted for clams and seaweeds, though he
pretended to be a very terrible person. Naturally the
Chickies and the Gooverooskies and the Epatkas, the
Burgomaster Gulls and the Kittiwakes and the Puffins,
who are always looking for a chance to be rude, took
up the cry, and—so Limmershin told me—for nearly

five minutes you could not have heard a gun fired on
Walrus Islet. All the population was yelling and
screaming: "Clam-eater! *Stareek* [old man]!" while
Sea Vitch rolled from side to side grunting and cough-
ing.

"*Now* will you tell?" said Kotick, all out of breath.

"Go and ask Sea Cow," said Sea Vitch. "If he is
living still, he'll be able to tell you."

"How shall I know Sea Cow when I meet him?"
said Kotick, sheering off.

"He's the only thing in the sea uglier than Sea
Vitch," screamed a burgomaster gull, wheeling under
Sea Vitch's nose. "Uglier, and with worse manners!
Stareek!"

Kotick swam back to Novastoshnah, leaving the
gulls to scream. There he found that no one sympa-
thised with him in his little attempts to discover a quiet
place for the seals. They told him that men had always
driven the holluschickie—it was part of the day's work
—and that if he did not like to see ugly things he should
not have gone to the killing-grounds. But none of the
other seals had seen the killing, and that made the difference between him and his friends. Besides, Kotick
was a white seal.

"What you must do," said old Sea Catch, after he
had heard his son's adventures, "is to grow up and be
a big seal like your father, and have a nursery on the
beach, and then they will leave you alone. In another
five years you ought to be able to fight for yourself."
Even gentle Matkah, his mother, said: "You will never
be able to stop the killing. Go and play in the sea,
Kotick." And Kotick went off and danced the Fire-
dance with a very heavy little heart.

That autumn he left the beach as soon as he could,
and set off alone because of a notion in his bullet-head.

He was going to find Sea Cow, if there was such a person in the sea, and he was going to find a quiet island with good firm beaches for seals to live on, where men could not get at them. So he explored and explored by himself from the North to the South Pacific, swimming as much as three hundred miles in a day and a night. He met with more adventures than can be told, and narrowly escaped being caught by the Basking Shark, and the Spotted Shark, and the Hammerhead, and he met all the untrustworthy ruffians that loaf up and down the seas, and the heavy polite fish, and the scarlet-spotted scallops that are moored in one place for hundreds of years, and grow very proud of it; but he never met Sea Cow, and he never found an island that he could fancy.

If the beach was good and hard, with a slope behind it for seals to play on, there was always the smoke of a whaler on the horizon, boiling down blubber, and Kotick knew what *that* meant. Or else he could see that seals had once visited the island and been killed off, and Kotick knew that where men had come once they would come again.

He picked up with an old stumpy-tailed albatross, who told him that Kerguelen Island was the very place for peace and quiet, and when Kotick went down there he was all but smashed to pieces against some wicked black cliffs in a heavy sleet-storm with lightning and thunder. Yet as he pulled out against the gale he could see that even there had once been a seal-nursery. And so it was in all the other islands that he visited.

Limmershin gave a long list of them, for he said that Kotick spent five seasons exploring, with a four months' rest each year at Novastoshnah, when the holluschickie used to make fun of him and his imaginary islands. He went to the Gallapagos, a horrid dry place on the Equator, where he was nearly baked to death; he went to the Georgia Islands, the South Orkneys, Emerald Island, Little Nightingale Island, Gough's Island, Bouvet's Island, the Crossets, and even to a little speck of an island south of the Cape of Good Hope. But everywhere the People of the Sea told him the same things. Seals had come to those islands once upon a time, but men had killed them all off. Even when he swam thousands of miles out of the Pacific, and got to a place called Cape Corrientes (that was when he was coming back from Gough's Island), he found a few hundred mangy seals on a rock, and they told him that men came there too.

That nearly broke his heart, and he headed round the Horn back to his own beaches; and on his way north he hauled out on an island full of green trees, where he found an old, old seal who was dying, and Kotick caught fish for him, and told him all his sorrows. "Now," said Kotick, "I am going back to Novastoshnah, and if I am driven to the killing-pens with the holluschickie I shall not care."

The old seal said: "Try once more. I am the last of the Lost Rookery of Masafuera, and in the days when men killed us by the hundred thousand there was a story on the beaches that some day a white seal would come out of the north and lead the seal people to a quiet place. I am old and I shall never live to see that day, but others will. Try once more."

And Kotick curled up his moustache (it was a beauty), and said: "I am the only white seal that has ever been born on the beaches, and I am the only seal, black or white, who ever thought of looking for new islands."

That cheered him immensely; and when he came

back to Novastoshnah that summer, Matkah, his
mother, begged him to marry and settle down, for he
was no longer a holluschick, but a full-grown sea-
catch, with a curly white mane on his shoulders, as
heavy, as big, and as fierce as his father. "Give me
another season," he said. "Remember, Mother, it is
always the seventh wave that goes farthest up the
beach."

Curiously enough, there was another seal who
thought that she would put off marrying till the next
year, and Kotick danced the Fire-dance with her all
down Lukannon Beach the night before he set off on
his last exploration.

This time he went westward, because he had fallen
on the trail of a great shoal of halibut, and he needed
at least one hundred pounds of fish a day to keep him
in good condition. He chased them till he was tired,
and then he curled himself up and went to sleep on the
hollows of the ground-swell that sets in to Copper
Island. He knew the coast perfectly well, so about
midnight, when he felt himself gently bumped on a
weed-bed, he said, "Hm, tide's running strong to-
night," and turning over under water opened his eyes
slowly and stretched. Then he jumped like a cat, for
he saw huge things nosing about in the shoal water
and browsing on the heavy fringes of the weeds.

"By the Great Combers of Magellan!" he said, beneath his moustache. "Who in the Deep Sea are these
people?"

They were like no walrus, sea-lion, seal, bear, whale,
shark, fish, squid, or scallop that Kotick had ever seen
before. They were between twenty and thirty feet
long, and they had no hind flippers, but a shovel-like
tail that looked as if it had been whittled out of wet
leather. Their heads were the most foolish-looking

things you ever saw, and they balanced on the ends of
their tails in deep water when they weren't grazing,
bowing solemnly to one another and waving their
front flippers as a fat man waves his arm.

"Ahem!" said Kotick. "Good sport, gentlemen?"
The big things answered by bowing and waving their
flippers like the Frog-Footman. When they began
feeding again Kotick saw that their upper lip was split
into two pieces that they could twitch apart about a
foot and bring together again with a whole bushel of
seaweed between the splits. They tucked the stuff into
their mouths and chumped solemnly.

"Messy style of feeding, that," said Kotick. They
bowed again, and Kotick began to lose his temper.
"Very good," he said. "If you do happen to have an
extra joint in your front flipper you needn't show off
so. I see you bow gracefully, but I should like to know
your names." The split lips moved and twitched, and
the glassy green eyes stared; but they did not speak.

"Well!" said Kotick, "you're the only people I've
ever met uglier than Sea Vitch—and with worse manners."

Then he remembered in a flash what the Burgomaster Gull had screamed to him when he was a little
yearling at Walrus Islet, and he tumbled backward in
the water, for he knew that he had found Sea Cow
at last.

The sea cows went on schlooping and grazing and
chumping in the weed, and Kotick asked them questions in every language that he had picked up in his
travels: and the Sea People talk nearly as many lan-
guages as human beings. But the Sea Cow did not
answer, because Sea Cow cannot talk. He has only six
bones in his neck where he ought to have seven, and
they say under the sea that that prevents him from

speaking even to his companions; but, as you know, he has an extra joint in his fore flipper, and by waving it up and down and about he makes a sort of clumsy telegraphic code.

By daylight Kotick's mane was standing on end and his temper was gone where the dead crabs go. Then the Sea Cow began to travel northward very slowly, stopping to hold absurd bowing councils from time to time, and Kotick followed them, saying to himself: "People who are such idiots as these are would have been killed long ago if they hadn't found out some safe island; and what is good enough for the Sea Cow is good enough for the Sea Catch. All the same, I wish they'd hurry."

It was weary work for Kotick. The herd never went more than forty or fifty miles a day, and stopped to feed at night, and kept close to the shore all the time; while Kotick swam round them, and over them, and under them, but he could not hurry them on one half-mile. As they went farther north they held a bowing council every few hours, and Kotick nearly bit off his moustache with impatience till he saw that they were following up a warm current of water, and then he respected them more.

One night they sank through the shiny water—sank like stones—and, for the first time since he had known them, began to swim quickly. Kotick followed, and the pace astonished him, for he never dreamed that Sea Cow was anything of a swimmer. They headed for a cliff by the shore—a cliff that ran down into deep water, and plunged into a dark hole at the foot of it, twenty fathoms under the sea. It was a long, long swim, and Kotick badly wanted fresh air before he was out of the dark tunnel that they led him through.

"My wig!" he said, when he rose, gasping and puffing, into open water at the farther end. "It was a long dive, but it was worth it."

The sea cows had separated, and were browsing lazily along the edges of the finest beaches that Kotick had ever seen. There were long stretches of smoothworn rock running for miles, exactly fitted to make seal-nurseries, and there were playgrounds of hard sand sloping inland behind them, and there were rollers for seals to dance in, and long grass to roll in, and sand-dunes to climb up and down; and, best of all, Kotick knew by the feel of the water, which never deceives a true Sea Catch, that no men had ever come there.

The first thing he did was to assure himself that the fishing was good, and then he swam along the beaches and counted up the delightful low sandy islands half hidden in the beautiful rolling fog. Away to the northward out to sea ran a line of bars and shoals and rocks that would never let a ship come within six miles of the beach; and between the islands and the mainland was a stretch of deep water that ran up to the perpendicular cliffs, and somewhere below the cliffs was the mouth of the tunnel.

"It's Novastoshnah over again, but ten times better," said Kotick. "Sea Cow must be wiser than I thought. Men can't come down the cliffs, even if there were any men; and the shoals to seaward would knock a ship to splinters. If any place in the sea is safe, this is it."

He began to think of the seal he had left behind him, but though he was in a hurry to go back to Novastoshnah, he thoroughly explored the new country, so that he would be able to answer all questions.

Then he dived and made sure of the mouth of the tunnel, and raced through to the southward. No one but a sea cow or a seal would have dreamed of there being such a place, and when he looked back at the cliffs even Kotick could hardly believe that he had been under them.

He was six days going home, though he was not swimming slowly; and when he hauled out just above Sea-Lion's Neck the first person he met was the seal who had been waiting for him, and she saw by the look in his eyes that he had found his island at last.

But the holluschickie and Sea Catch, his father, and all the other seals, laughed at him when he told them what he had discovered, and a young seal about his own age said: "This is all very well, Kotick, but you can't come from no one knows where and order us off like this. Remember we've been fighting for our nurseries, and that's a thing you never did. You preferred prowling about in the sea."

The other seals laughed at this, and the young seal began twisting his head from side to side. He had just married that year, and was making a great fuss about it.

"I've no nursery to fight for," said Kotick. "I want only to show you all a place where you will be safe. What's the use of fighting?"

"Oh, if you're trying to back out, of course I've no more to say," said the young seal, with an ugly chuckle.

"Will you come with me if I win?" said Kotick; and a green light came into his eyes, for he was very angry at having to fight at all.

"Very good," said the young seal carelessly. "*If* you win, I'll come."

He had no time to change his mind, for Kotick's head darted out and his teeth sunk in the blubber of the young seal's neck. Then he threw himself back on his haunches and hauled his enemy down the beach, shook him, and knocked him over. Then Kotick roared to the seals: "I've done my best for you these five seasons past. I've found you the island where you'll be safe, but unless your heads are dragged off your silly necks you won't believe. I'm going to teach you now. Look out for yourselves!"

Limmershin told me that never in his life—and Limmershin sees ten thousand big seals fighting every year —never in all his little life did he see anything like Kotick's charge into the nurseries. He flung himself at the biggest sea-catch he could find, caught him by the throat, choked him and bumped him and banged him till he grunted for mercy, and then threw him aside and attacked the next. You see, Kotick had never fasted for four months as the big seals did every year, and his deep-sea swimming-trips kept him in perfect condition, and, best of all, he had never fought before. His curly white mane stood up with rage, and his eyes flamed, and his big dog-teeth glistened, and he was splendid to look at.

Old Sea Catch, his father, saw him tearing past, hauling the grizzled old seals about as though they had been halibut, and upsetting the young bachelors in all directions; and Sea Catch gave one roar and shouted: "He may be a fool, but he is the best fighter on the Beaches. Don't tackle your father, my son! He's with you!"

Kotick roared in answer, and old Sea Catch waddled in, his moustache on end, blowing like a locomotive, while Matkah and the seal that was going to marry Kotick cowered down and admired their menfolk. It was a gorgeous fight, for the two fought as long as there was a seal that dared lift up his head, and then they paraded grandly up and down the beach side by side, bellowing.

At night, just as the Northern Lights were winking and flashing through the fog, Kotick climbed a bare rock and looked down on the scattered nurseries and the torn and bleeding seals. "Now," he said, "I've taught you your lesson."

"My wig!" said old Sea Catch, boosting himself up stiffly, for he was fearfully mauled. "The Killer Whale himself could not have cut them up worse. Son, I'm proud of you, and what's more, *I'll* come with you to your island—if there is such a place."

"Here you, fat pigs of the sea! Who comes with me to the Sea Cow's tunnel? Answer, or I shall teach you again," roared Kotick.

There was a murmur like the ripple of the tide all up and down the beaches. "We will come," said thousands of tired voices. "We will follow Kotick, the White Seal."

Then Kotick dropped his head between his shoulders and shut his eyes proudly. He was not a white seal any more, but red from head to tail. All the same, he would have scorned to look at or touch one of his wounds.

A week later he and his army (nearly ten thousand holluschickie and old seals) went away north to the Sea Cow's tunnel, Kotick leading them, and the seals that stayed at Novastoshnah called them idiots. But next spring, when they all met off the fishing-banks of the Pacific, Kotick's seals told such tales of the new beaches beyond Sea Cow's tunnel that more and more seals left Novastoshnah.

Of course it was not all done at once, for the seals need a long time to turn things over in their minds, but year by year more seals went away from Novastoshnah, and Lukannon, and the other nurseries, to the quiet, sheltered beaches where Kotick sits all the summer through, getting bigger and fatter and stronger each year, while the holluschickie play round him, in that sea where no man comes.

". . . BETWEEN THE ISLANDS AND THE MAINLAND WAS A STRETCH OF DEEP WATER THAT RAN UP TO THE PERPENDICULAR CLIFFS . . ." (*page* 47)

LUKANNON

This is the great deep-sea song that all the St. Paul seals sing when they are heading back to their beaches in the summer. It is a sort of very sad seal National Anthem.

I met my mates in the morning (and oh, but I am old!)
Where roaring on the ledges the summer ground-swell
*   rolled;*
I heard them lift the chorus that drowned the breakers'
*   song—*
The Beaches of Lukannon—two million voices strong!

The song of pleasant stations beside the salt lagoons,
The song of blowing squadrons that shuffled down
    the dunes,
The song of midnight dances that churned the sea to
    flame—
The Beaches of Lukannon—before the sealers came!

I met my mates in the morning (I'll never meet them
*   more!);*
They came and went in legions that darkened all the
*   shore.*
And through the foam-flecked offing as far as voice
*   could reach*
We hailed the landing-parties and we sang them up
*   the beach.*

The Beaches of Lukannon—the winter-wheat so tall—
The dripping, crinkled lichens, and the sea-fog
    drenching all!
The platforms of our playground, all shining smooth
    and worn!
The Beaches of Lukannon—the home where we were
    born!

*I meet my mates in the morning, a broken, scattered
    band.*
Men shoot us in the water and club us on the land;
*Men drive us to the Salt House like silly sheep and
    tame,*
And still we sing Lukannon—before the sealers came.

Wheel down, wheel down to southward! Oh
    Gooverooska go!
And tell the Deep-Sea Viceroys the story of our woe;
Ere, empty as the shark's egg the tempest flings ashore,
The Beaches of Lukannon shall know their sons no
    more!

THE MIRACLE OF
PURUN BHAGAT

THE MIRACLE OF PURUN BHAGAT

The night we felt the earth would move
 We stole and plucked him by the hand,
Because we loved him with the love
 That knows but cannot understand.

And when the roaring hillside broke,
 And all our world fell down in rain,
We saved him, we the Little Folk;
 But lo! he does not come again!

Mourn now, we saved him for the sake
 Of such poor love as wild ones may.
Mourn ye! Our brother will not wake,
 And his own kind drive us away!

Dirge of the Langurs

THERE WAS once a man in India who was Prime
Minister of one of the semi-independent native States
in the north-western part of the country. He was a
Brahmin, so high-caste that caste ceased to have any
particular meaning for him; and his father had been
an important official in the gay-coloured tag-rag and
bobtail of an old-fashioned Hindu Court. But as Purun
Dass grew up he felt that the old order of things was

changing, and that if any one wished to get on in the
world he must stand well with the English, and imitate
all that the English believed to be good. At the same
time a native official must keep his own master's favour. This was a difficult game, but the quiet, close-
mouthed young Brahmin, helped by a good English
education at a Bombay University, played it coolly,
and rose, step by step, to be Prime Minister of the king-
dom. That is to say, he held more real power than his
master, the Maharajah.

When the old king—who was suspicious of the
English, their railways and telegraphs—died, Purun
Dass stood high with his young successor, who had
been tutored by an Englishman; and between them,
though he always took care that his master should have
the credit, they established schools for little girls, made
roads, and started State dispensaries and shows of agri-
cultural implements, and published a yearly blue-book
on the "Moral and Material Progress of the State," and
the Foreign Office and the Government of India were
delighted. Very few native States take up English
progress altogether, for they will not believe, as Purun
Dass showed he did, that what was good for the Englishman must be twice as good for the Asiatic. The
Prime Minister became the honoured friend of Viceroys, and Governors, and Lieutenant-Governors, and
medical missionaries, and common missionaries, and
hard-riding English officers who came to shoot in the
State preserves, as well as of whole hosts of tourists
who travelled up and down India in the cold weather,
showing how things ought to be managed. In his spare
time he would endow scholarships for the study of
medicine and manufactures on strictly English lines,
and write letters to the *Pioneer*, the greatest Indian
daily paper, explaining his master's aims and objects.

At last he went to England on a visit, and had to pay enormous sums to the priests when he came back; for even so high-caste a Brahmin as Purun Dass lost caste by crossing the black sea. In London he met and talked with every one worth knowing—men whose names go all over the world—and saw a great deal more than he said. He was given honorary degrees by learned universities, and he made speeches and talked of Hindu social reform to English ladies in evening dress, till all London cried, "This is the most fascinating man we have ever met at dinner since cloths were first laid."

When he returned to India there was a blaze of glory, for the Viceroy himself made a special visit to confer upon the Maharajah the Grand Cross of the Star of India—all diamonds and ribbons and enamel; and at the same ceremony, while the cannon boomed, Purun Dass was made a Knight Commander of the Order of the Indian Empire; so that his name stood Sir Purun Dass, K.C.I.E.

That evening, at dinner in the big Viceregal tent, he stood up with the badge and the collar of the Order on his breast, and replying to the toast of his master's health, made a speech few Englishmen could have bettered.

Next month, when the city had returned to its sun-baked quiet, he did a thing no Englishman would have dreamed of doing; for, so far as the world's affairs went, he died. The jewelled order of his knighthood went back to the Indian Government, and a new Prime Minister was appointed to the charge of affairs, and a great game of General Post began in all the subordinate appointments. The priests knew what had happened, and the people guessed; but India is the one place in the world where a man can do as he pleases and nobody asks why; and the fact that Dewan Sir Purun

Dass, K.C.I.E., had resigned position, palace, and power, and taken up the begging-bowl and ochre-coloured dress of a Sunnyasi, or holy man, was considered nothing extraordinary. He had been, as the Old Law recommends, twenty years a youth, twenty years a fighter,—though he had never carried a weapon in his life,—and twenty years head of a household. He had used his wealth and his power for what he knew both to be worth; he had taken honour when it came his way; he had seen men and cities far and near, and men and cities had stood up and honoured him. Now he would let these things go, as a man drops the cloak he no longer needs.

Behind him, as he walked through the city gates, an antelope skin and brass-handled crutch under his arm, and a begging-bowl of polished brown *coco-de-mer* in his hand, barefoot, alone, with eyes cast on the ground—behind him they were firing salutes from the bastions in honour of his happy successor. Purun Dass nodded. All that life was ended; and he bore it no more ill-will or good-will than a man bears to a colourless dream of the night. He was a Sunnyasi—a houseless, wandering mendicant, depending on his neighbours for his daily bread; and so long as there is a morsel to divide in India, neither priest nor beggar starves. He had never in his life tasted meat, and very seldom eaten even fish. A five-pound note would have covered his personal expenses for food through any one of the many years in which he had been absolute master of millions of money. Even when he was being lionised in London he had held before him his dream of peace and quiet—the long, white, dusty Indian road, printed all over with bare feet, the incessant, slow-moving traffic, and the sharp-smelling wood smoke curling up under the fig-trees in the twilight, where the wayfarers sit at their evening meal.

When the time came to make that dream true the Prime Minister took the proper steps, and in three days you might more easily have found a bubble in the trough of the long Atlantic seas than Purun Dass among the roving, gathering, separating millions of India.

At night his antelope skin was spread where the darkness overtook him—sometimes in a Sunnyasi monastery by the roadside; sometimes by a mud-pillar shrine of Kala Pir, where the Jogis, who are another misty division of holy men, would receive him as they do those who know what castes and divisions are worth; sometimes on the outskirts of a little Hindu village, where the children would steal up with the food their parents had prepared; and sometimes on the pitch of the bare grazing-grounds, where the flame of his stick fire waked the drowsy camels. It was all one to Purun Dass—or Purun Bhagat, as he called himself now. Earth, people, and food were all one. But unconsciously his feet drew him away northward and eastward; from the south to Rohtak; from Rohtak to Kurnool; from Kurnool to ruined Samanah, and then up-stream along the dried bed of the Gugger river that fills only when the rain falls in the hills, till one day he saw the far line of the great Himalayas.

Then Purun Bhagat smiled, for he remembered that his mother was of Rajput Brahmin birth, from Kulu way—a Hill-woman, always home-sick for the snows—and that the least touch of Hill blood draws a man in the end back to where he belongs.

"Yonder," said Purun Bhagat, breasting the lower slopes of the Sewaliks, where the cacti stand up like seven-branched candlesticks—"yonder I shall sit down and get knowledge"; and the cool wind of the Himalayas whistled about his ears as he trod the road that led to Simla.

The last time he had come that way it had been in
state, with a clattering cavalry escort, to visit the
gentlest and most affable of Viceroys; and the two had
talked for an hour together about mutual friends in
London, and what the Indian common folk really
thought of things. This time Purun Bhagat paid no
calls, but leaned on the rail of the Mall, watching that
glorious view of the plains spread out forty miles below, till a native Mohammedan policeman told him
he was obstructing traffic; and Purun Bhagat salaamed
reverently to the Law, because he knew the value of
it, and was seeking for a Law of his own. Then he
moved on, and slept that night in an empty hut at
Chota Simla, which looks like the very last end of the
earth, but it was only the beginning of his journey.

He followed the Himalaya-Thibet road, the little
ten-foot track that is blasted out of solid rock, or
strutted out on timbers over gulfs a thousand feet deep;
that dips into warm, wet, shut-in valleys, and climbs
out across bare, grassy hill-shoulders where the sun
strikes like a burning-glass; or turns through dripping,
dark forests where the tree-ferns dress the trunks from
head to heel, and the pheasant calls to his mate. And he
met Thibetan herdsmen with their dogs and flocks
of sheep, each sheep with a little bag of borax on his
back, and wandering wood-cutters, and cloaked and
blanketed Lamas from Thibet, coming into India on
pilgrimage, and envoys of little solitary Hill-states,
posting furiously on ring-streaked and piebald ponies,
or the cavalcade of a Rajah paying a visit; or else for
a long, clear day he would see nothing more than a
black bear grunting and rooting below in the valley.
When he first started, the roar of the world he had left
still rang in his ears, as the roar of a tunnel rings long
after the train has passed through; but when he had
put the Mutteeanee Pass behind him that was all done,

and Purun Bhagat was alone with himself, walking, wondering, and thinking, his eyes on the ground, and his thoughts with the clouds.

One evening he crossed the highest pass he had met till then—it had been a two-days' climb—and came out on a line of snow-peaks that banded all the horizon—mountains from fifteen to twenty thousand feet high, looking almost near enough to hit with a stone, though they were fifty or sixty miles away. The pass was crowned with dense, dark forest—deodar, walnut, wild cherry, wild olive, and wild pear, but mostly deodar, which is the Himalayan cedar; and under the shadow of the deodars stood a deserted shrine to Kali—who is Durga, who is Sitala, who is sometimes worshipped against the smallpox.

Purun Dass swept the stone floor clean, smiled at the grinning statue, made himself a little mud fireplace at the back of the shrine, spread his antelope skin on a bed of fresh pine-needles, tucked his *bairagi*—his brass-handled crutch—under his armpit, and sat down to rest.

Immediately below him the hillside fell away, clean and cleared for fifteen hundred feet, where a little village of stone-walled houses, with roofs of beaten earth, clung to the steep tilt. All round it the tiny ter-raced fields lay out like aprons of patchwork on the knees of the mountain, and cows no bigger than beetles grazed between the smooth stone circles of the threshing-floors. Looking across the valley, the eye was deceived by the size of things, and could not at first realise that what seemed to be low scrub, on the opposite mountain-flank, was in truth a forest of hun-dred-foot pines. Purun Bhagat saw an eagle swoop across the gigantic hollow, but the great bird dwindled to a dot ere it was half-way over. A few bands of scat-

tered clouds strung up and down the valley, catching
on a shoulder of the hills, or rising up and dying out
when they were level with the head of the pass. And
"Here shall I find peace," said Purun Bhagat.

Now, a Hill-man makes nothing of a few hundred
feet up or down, and as soon as the villagers saw the
smoke in the deserted shrine, the village priest climbed
up the terraced hillside to welcome the stranger.

When he met Purun Bhagat's eyes—the eyes of a
man used to control thousands—he bowed to the earth,
took the begging-bowl without a word, and returned
to the village, saying, "We have at last a holy man.
Never have I seen such a man. He is of the Plains—but
pale-coloured—a Brahmin of the Brahmins." Then all
the housewives of the village said, "Think you he will
stay with us?" and each did her best to cook the most
savoury meal for the Bhagat. Hill-food is very simple,
but with buckwheat and Indian corn, and rice and red
pepper, and little fish out of the stream in the valley,
and honey from the flue-like hives built in the stone
walls, and dried apricots, and turmeric, and wild gin-
ger, and bannocks of flour, a devout woman can make
good things, and it was a full bowl that the priest carried to the Bhagat. Was he going to stay? asked the
priest. Would he need a *chela*—a disciple—to beg for
him? Had he a blanket against the cold weather? Was
the food good?

Purun Bhagat ate, and thanked the giver. It was in
his mind to stay. That was sufficient, said the priest.
Let the begging-bowl be placed outside the shrine, in
the hollow made by those two twisted roots, and daily
should the Bhagat be fed; for the village felt honoured
that such a man—he looked timidly into the Bhagat's
face—should tarry among them.

That day saw the end of Purun Bhagat's wanderings.

He had come to the place appointed for him—the silence and the space. After this, time stopped, and he, sitting at the mouth of the shrine, could not tell whether he were alive or dead; a man with control of his limbs, or a part of the hills, and the clouds, and the shifting rain and sunlight. He would repeat a Name softly to himself a hundred hundred times, till, at each repetition, he seemed to move more and more out of his body, sweeping up to the doors of some tremendous discovery; but, just as the door was opening, his body would drag him back, and, with grief, he felt he was locked up again in the flesh and bones of Purun Bhagat.

Every morning the filled begging-bowl was laid silently in the crutch of the roots outside the shrine. Sometimes the priest brought it; sometimes a Ladakhi trader, lodging in the village, and anxious to get merit, trudged up the path; but, more often, it was the woman who had cooked the meal overnight; and she would murmur, hardly above her breath: "Speak for me before the gods, Bhagat. Speak for such a one, the wife of so-and-so!" Now and then some bold child would be allowed the honour, and Purun Bhagat would hear him drop the bowl and run as fast as his little legs could carry him, but the Bhagat never came down to the village. It was laid out like a map at his feet. He could see the evening gatherings held on the circle of the threshing-floors, because that was the only level ground; could see the wonderful unnamed green of the young rice, the indigo blues of the Indian corn, the dock-like patches of buckwheat, and, in its season, the red bloom of the amaranth, whose tiny seeds, being neither grain nor pulse, make a food that can be lawfully eaten by Hindus in time of fasts.

When the year turned, the roofs of the huts were all little squares of purest gold, for it was on the roofs that they laid out their cobs of the corn to dry. Hiving and harvest, rice-sowing and husking, passed before his eyes, all embroidered down there on the many-sided plots of fields, and he thought of them all, and wondered what they all led to at the long last.

Even in populated India a man cannot a day sit still before the wild things run over him as though he were a rock; and in that wilderness very soon the wild things, who knew Kali's Shrine well, came back to look at the intruder. The *langurs*, the big gray-whiskered monkeys of the Himalayas, were, naturally, the first, for they are alive with curiosity; and when they had upset the begging-bowl, and rolled it round the floor, and tried their teeth on the brass-handled crutch, and made faces at the antelope skin, they decided that the human being who sat so still was harmless. At evening, they would leap down from the pines, and beg with their hands for things to eat, and then swing off in graceful curves. They liked the warmth of the fire, too, and huddled round it till Purun Bhagat had to push them aside to throw on more fuel; and in the morning, as

often as not, he would find a furry ape sharing his
blanket. All day long, one or other of the tribe would
sit by his side, staring out at the snows, crooning and
looking unspeakably wise and sorrowful.

After the monkeys came the *barasingh*, that big deer
which is like our red deer, but stronger. He wished to
rub off the velvet of his horns against the cold stones
of Kali's statue, and stamped his feet when he saw the
man at the shrine. But Purun Bhagat never moved,
and, little by little, the royal stag edged up and nuzzled
his shoulder. Purun Bhagat slid one cool hand along the
hot antlers, and the touch soothed the fretted beast,
who bowed his head, and Purun Bhagat very softly
rubbed and ravelled off the velvet. Afterward, the
barasingh brought his doe and fawn—gentle things that
mumbled on the holy man's blanket—or would come
alone at night, his eyes green in the fire-flicker, to take
his share of fresh walnuts. At last, the musk-deer, the
shyest and almost the smallest of the deerlets, came,
too, her big rabbity ears erect; even brindled, silent
mushick-nabha must needs find out what the light in
the shrine meant, and drop out her moose-like nose
into Purun Bhagat's lap, coming and going with the
shadows of the fire. Purun Bhagat called them all "my
brothers," and his low call of *"Bhai! Bhai!"* would
draw them from the forest at noon if they were within
earshot. The Himalayan black bear, moody and suspicious—Sona, who has the V-shaped white mark under his chin—passed that way more than once; and
since the Bhagat showed no fear, Sona showed no
anger, but watched him, and came closer, and begged
a share of the caresses, and a dole of bread or wild ber-
ries. Often, in the still dawns, when the Bhagat would
climb to the very crest of the pass to watch the red day
walking along the peaks of the snows, he would find

". . . WHAT HAD BEEN FOREST . . . WAS NOW ONE RAW, RED
FAN-SHAPED SMEAR . . ." (*page 72*)

Sona shuffling and grunting at his heels, thrusting a curious fore-paw under fallen trunks, and bringing it away with a *whoof* of impatience; or his early steps would wake Sona where he lay curled up, and the great brute, rising erect, would think to fight, till he heard the Bhagat's voice and knew his best friend.

Nearly all hermits and holy men who live apart from the big cities have the reputation of being able to work miracles with the wild things, but all the miracle lies in keeping still, in never making a hasty movement, and, for a long time, at least, in never looking directly at a visitor. The villagers saw the outline of the *barasingh* stalking like a shadow through the dark forest behind the shrine; saw the *minaul*, the Himalayan pheasant, blazing in her best colours before Kali's statue; and the *langurs* on their haunches, inside, playing with the walnut shells. Some of the children, too, had heard Sona singing to himself, bear-fashion, behind the fallen rocks, and the Bhagat's reputation as miracle-worker stood firm.

Yet nothing was farther from his mind than miracles. He believed that all things were one big Miracle, and when a man knows that much he knows something to go upon. He knew for a certainty that there was nothing great and nothing little in this world: and day and night he strove to think out his way into the heart of things, back to the place whence his soul had come.

So thinking, his untrimmed hair fell down about his shoulders, the stone slab at the side of the antelope skin was dented into a little hole by the foot of his brass-handled crutch, and the place between the tree-trunks, where the begging-bowl rested day after day, sunk and wore into a hollow almost as smooth as the brown shell itself; and each beast knew his exact place at the fire. The fields changed their colours with the

seasons; the threshing-floors filled and emptied, and
filled again and again; and again and again, when winter came, the *langurs* frisked among the branches feath-
ered with light snow, till the mother-monkeys brought
their sad-eyed little babies up from the warmer valleys
with the spring. There were few changes in the village.
The priest was older, and many of the little children
who used to come with the begging-dish sent their
own children now; and when you asked of the villagers how long their holy man had lived in Kali's
Shrine at the head of the pass, they answered, "Always."

Then came such summer rains as had not been
known in the Hills for many seasons. Through three
good months the valley was wrapped in cloud and
soaking mist—steady, unrelenting downfall, breaking
off into thunder-shower after thunder-shower. Kali's
Shrine stood above the clouds, for the most part, and
there was a whole month in which the Bhagat never
caught a glimpse of his village. It was packed away
under a white floor of cloud that swayed and shifted
and rolled on itself and bulged upward, but never
broke from its piers—the streaming flanks of the valley.

All that time he heard nothing but the sound of a
million little waters, overhead from the trees, and
underfoot along the ground, soaking through the pine-
needles, dripping from the tongues of draggled fern,
and spouting in newly-torn muddy channels down
the slopes. Then the sun came out, and drew forth the
good incense of the deodars and the rhododendrons,
and that far-off, clean smell which the Hill people call
"the smell of the snows." The hot sunshine lasted for
a week, and then the rains gathered together for their
last downpour, and the water fell in sheets that flayed
off the skin of the ground and leaped back in mud.

Purun Bhagat heaped his fire high that night, for he was sure his brothers would need warmth; but never a beast came to the shrine, though he called and called till he dropped asleep, wondering what had happened in the woods.

It was in the black heart of the night, the rain drumming like a thousand drums, that he was roused by a plucking at his blanket, and, stretching out, felt the little hand of a *langur*. "It is better here than in the trees," he said sleepily, loosening a fold of blanket; "take it and be warm." The monkey caught his hand and pulled hard. "Is it food, then?" said Purun Bhagat. "Wait awhile, and I will prepare some." As he kneeled to throw fuel on the fire the *langur* ran to the door of the shrine, crooned, and ran back again, plucking at the man's knee.

"What is it? What is thy trouble, Brother?" said Purun Bhagat, for the *langur's* eyes were full of things that he could not tell. "Unless one of thy caste be in a trap—and none set traps here—I will not go into that weather. Look, Brother, even the *barasingh* comes for shelter!"

The deer's antlers clashed as he strode into the shrine, clashed against the grinning statue of Kali. He lowered them in Purun Bhagat's direction and stamped uneasily, hissing through his half-shut nostrils.

"Hai! Hai! Hai!" said the Bhagat, snapping his fingers. "Is *this* payment for a night's lodging?" But the deer pushed him toward the door, and as he did so Purun Bhagat heard the sound of something opening with a sigh, and saw two slabs of the floor draw away from each other, while the sticky earth below smacked its lips.

"Now I see," said Purun Bhagat. "No blame to my brothers that they did not sit by the fire to-night. The mountain is falling. And yet—why should I go?" His eye fell on the empty begging-bowl, and his face changed. "They have given me good food daily since— since I came, and, if I am not swift, to-morrow there will not be one mouth in the valley. Indeed, I must go and warn them below. Back there, Brother! Let me get to the fire."

The *barasingh* backed unwillingly as Purun Bhagat drove a pine torch deep into the flame, twirling it till it was well lit. "Ah! ye came to warn me," he said, rising. "Better than that we shall do; better than that. Out, now, and lend me thy neck, Brother, for I have but two feet."

He clutched the bristling withers of the *barasingh* with his right hand, held the torch away with his left, and stepped out of the shrine into the desperate night. There was no breath of wind, but the rain nearly drowned the flare as the great deer hurried down the slope, sliding on his haunches. As soon as they were clear of the forest more of the Bhagat's brothers joined them. He heard, though he could not see, the *langurs* pressing about him, and behind them the *uhh! uhh!* of Sona. The rain matted his long white hair into ropes; the water splashed beneath his bare feet, and his yellow robe clung to his frail old body, but he stepped down steadily, leaning against the *barasingh*. He was no longer a holy man, but Sir Purun Dass, K.C.I.E., Prime Minister of no small State, a man accustomed to command, going out to save life. Down the steep, plashy path they poured all together, the Bhagat and his brothers, down and down till the deer's feet clicked and stumbled on the wall of a threshing-floor, and he snorted because he smelt Man. Now they were at the head of the one crooked village street, and the Bhagat beat with his crutch on the barred windows of the blacksmith's house, as his torch blazed up in the shelter of the eaves. "Up and out!" cried Purun Bhagat; and he did not know his own voice, for it was years since he had spoken aloud to a man. "The hill falls! The hill is falling! Up and out, oh, you within!"

"It is our Bhagat," said the blacksmith's wife. "He stands among his beasts. Gather the little ones and give the call."

It ran from house to house, while the beasts, cramped in the narrow way, surged and huddled round the Bhagat, and Sona puffed impatiently.

The people hurried into the street—they were no more than seventy souls all told—and in the glare of the torches they saw their Bhagat holding back the terrified *barasingh*, while the monkeys plucked piteously at his skirts, and Sona sat on his haunches and roared.

"Across the valley and up the next hill!" shouted Purun Bhagat. "Leave none behind! We follow!"

Then the people ran as only Hill folk can run, for they knew that in a landslip you must climb for the highest ground across the valley. They fled, splashing through the little river at the bottom, and panted up the terraced fields on the far side, while the Bhagat and his brethren followed. Up and up the opposite mountain they climbed, calling to each other by name—the roll-call of the village—and at their heels toiled the big *barasingh*, weighted by the failing strength of Purun Bhagat. At last the deer stopped in the shadow of a deep pine-wood, five hundred feet up the hillside. His instinct, that had warned him of the coming slide, told him he would be safe here.

Purun Bhagat dropped fainting by his side, for the chill of the rain and that fierce climb were killing him; but first he called to the scattered torches ahead, "Stay and count your numbers"; then, whispering to the deer as he saw the lights gather in a cluster: "Stay with me, Brother. Stay—till—I—go!"

There was a sigh in the air that grew to a mutter, and a mutter that grew to a roar, and a roar that passed all sense of hearing, and the hillside on which the villagers stood was hit in the darkness, and rocked to the blow. Then a note as steady, deep, and true as the deep C of the organ drowned everything for perhaps five minutes, while the very roots of the pines quivered to it. It died away, and the sound of the rain falling on miles of hard ground and grass changed to the muffled drum of water on soft earth. That told its own tale.

Never a villager—not even the priest—was bold enough to speak to the Bhagat who had saved their lives. They crouched under the pines and waited till the day. When it came they looked across the valley and saw that what had been forest, and terraced field, and track-threaded grazing-ground was one raw, red, fan-shaped smear, with a few trees flung head-down on the scarp. That red ran high up the hill of their refuge, damming back the little river, which had begun to spread into a brick-coloured lake. Of the village, of the road to the shrine, of the shrine itself, and the forest behind, there was no trace. For one mile in width and two thousand feet in sheer depth the mountain-side had come away bodily, planed clean from head to heel.

And the villagers, one by one, crept through the wood to pray before their Bhagat. They saw the *barasingh* standing over him, who fled when they came near, and they heard the *langurs* wailing in the branches, and Sona moaning up the hill; but their Bhagat was dead, sitting cross-legged, his back against a tree, his crutch under his armpit, and his face turned to the north-east.

The priest said: "Behold a miracle after a miracle, for in this very attitude must all Sunnyasis be buried! Therefore where he is now we will build the temple to our holy man."

They built the temple before a year was ended—a little stone-and-earth shrine—and they called the hill the Bhagat's hill, and they worship there with lights and flowers and offerings to this day. But they do not know that the saint of their worship is the late Sir Purun Dass, K.C.I.E., D.C.L., Ph.D., etc., once Prime Minister of the progressive and enlightened State of Mohiniwala, and honorary or corresponding member of more learned and scientific societies than will ever do any good in this world or the next.

A SONG OF KABIR

Oh, light was the world that he weighed in his hands!
Oh, heavy the tale of his fiefs and his lands!
He has gone from the guddee and put on the shroud,
And departed in guise of bairagi avowed!

Now the white road to Delhi is mat for his feet,
The sal and the kikar must guard him from heat;
His home is the camp, and the waste, and the crowd—
He is seeking the Way as bairagi avowed!

He has looked upon Man, and his eyeballs are clear
(There was One; there is One, and but One, saith
    Kabir);
The Red Mist of Doing has thinned to a cloud—
He has taken the Path for bairagi avowed!

To learn and discern of his brother the clod,
Of his brother the brute, and his brother the God.
He has gone from the council and put on the shroud
("Can ye hear?" saith Kabir), a bairagi avowed!

THE
UNDERTAKERS

THE UNDERTAKERS

*When ye say to Tabaqui, "My Brother!" when ye call
the Hyena to meat,
Ye may cry the Full Truce with Jacala—the Belly that
runs on four feet.*

Jungle Law

"RESPECT the aged!"

It was a thick voice—a muddy voice that would have
made you shudder—a voice like something soft breaking in two. There was a quaver in it, a croak and a
whine.

"Respect the aged! O Companions of the River—
respect the aged!"

Nothing could be seen on the broad reach of the
river except a little fleet of square-sailed, wooden-
pinned barges, loaded with building-stone, that had
just come under the railway bridge, and were driving
down-stream. They put their clumsy helms over to
avoid the sand-bar made by the scour of the bridge-
piers, and as they passed, three abreast, the horrible
voice began again:

"O Brahmins of the River—respect the aged and
infirm!"

A boatman turned where he sat on the gunwale,

lifted up his hand, said something that was not a bless-
ing, and the boats creaked on through the twilight.
The broad Indian river, that looked more like a chain
of little lakes than a stream, was as smooth as glass, re-
flecting the sandy-red sky in mid-channel, but splashed
with patches of yellow and dusky purple near and
under the low banks. Little creeks ran into the river
in the wet season, but now their dry mouths hung
clear above water-line. On the left shore, and almost
under the railway bridge, stood a mud-and-brick and
thatch-and-stick village, whose main street, full of
cattle going back to their byres, ran straight to the
river, and ended in a sort of rude brick pier-head,
where people who wanted to wash could wade in step
by step. That was the Ghaut of the village of Mugger-
Ghaut.

Night was falling fast over the fields of lentils and
rice and cotton in the low-lying ground yearly flooded
by the river; over the reeds that fringed the elbow of
the bend, and the tangled jungle of the grazing-
grounds behind the still reeds. The parrots and crows,
who had been chattering and shouting over their evening drink, had flown inland to roost, crossing the
out-going battalions of the flying-foxes; and cloud
upon cloud of water-birds came whistling and "honk-
ing" to the cover of the reed-beds. There were geese,
barrel-headed and black-backed, teal, widgeon, mal-
lard, and sheldrake, with curlews, and here and there
a flamingo.

A lumbering Adjutant-crane brought up the rear,
flying as though each slow stroke would be his last.

"Respect the aged! Brahmins of the River—respect
the aged!"

The Adjutant half turned his head, sheered a little
in the direction of the voice, and landed stiffly on the

sand-bar below the bridge. Then you saw what a
ruffianly brute he really was. His back view was immensely respectable, for he stood nearly six feet high,
and looked rather like a very proper bald-headed person. In front it was different, for his Ally Sloper-like
head and neck had not a feather to them, and there was
a horrible raw-skin pouch on his neck under his chin—
a hold-all for the things his pick-axe beak might steal.
His legs were long and thin and skinny, but he moved
them delicately, and looked at them with pride as he
preened down his ashy-gray tail-feathers, glanced over
the smooth of his shoulder, and stiffened into "Stand
at attention."

A mangy little Jackal, who had been yapping hungrily on a low bluff, cocked up his ears and tail, and
scuttered across the shallows to join the Adjutant.

He was the lowest of his caste—not that the best of
jackals are good for much, but this one was peculiarly
low, being half a beggar, half a criminal—a cleaner-up
of village rubbish-heaps, desperately timid or wildly
bold, everlastingly hungry, and full of cunning that
never did him any good.

"Ugh!" he said, shaking himself dolefully as he
landed. "May the red mange destroy the dogs of this
village! I have three bites for each flea upon me, and
all because I looked—only looked, mark you—at an old
shoe in a cow-byre. Can I eat mud?" He scratched
himself under his left ear.

"I heard," said the Adjutant, in a voice like a blunt
saw going through a thick board—"I *heard* there was
a new-born puppy in that same shoe."

"To hear is one thing; to know is another," said the
Jackal, who had a very fair knowledge of proverbs,
picked up by listening to men round the village fires
of an evening.

"Quite true. So, to make sure, I took care of that puppy while the dogs were busy elsewhere."

"They were *very* busy," said the Jackal. "Well, I must not go to the village hunting for scraps yet awhile. And so there truly was a blind puppy in that shoe?"

"It is here," said the Adjutant, squinting over his beak at his full pouch. "A small thing, but acceptable now that charity is dead in the world."

"Ahai! The world is iron in these days," wailed the Jackal. Then his restless eye caught the least possible ripple on the water, and he went on quickly: "Life is hard for us all, and I doubt not that even our excellent master, the Pride of the Ghaut and the Envy of the River——"

"A liar, a flatterer, and a Jackal were all hatched out of the same egg," said the Adjutant to nobody in particular; for he was rather a fine sort of a liar on his own account when he took the trouble.

"Yes, the Envy of the River," the Jackal repeated, raising his voice. "Even he, I doubt not, finds that since the bridge has been built good food is more scarce. But on the other hand, though I would by no means say this to his noble face, he is so wise and so virtuous —as I, alas! am not——"

"When the Jackal owns he is gray, how black must the Jackal be!" muttered the Adjutant. He could not see what was coming.

"That *his* food never fails, and in consequence——"

There was a soft grating sound, as though a boat had just touched in shoal water. The Jackal spun round quickly and faced (it is always best to face) the creature he had been talking about. It was a twenty-four-foot crocodile, cased in what looked like treble-riveted boiler-plate, studded and keeled and crested;

the yellow points of his upper teeth just overhanging his beautifully fluted lower jaw. It was the blunt-nosed Mugger of Mugger-Ghaut, older than any man in the village, who had given his name to the village; the demon of the ford before the railway bridge came—murderer, man-eater, and local fetish in one. He lay with his chin in the shallows, keeping his place by an almost invisible rippling of his tail, and well the Jackal knew that one stroke of that same tail in the water would carry the Mugger up the bank with the rush of a steam-engine.

"Auspiciously met, Protector of the Poor!" he fawned, backing at every word. "A delectable voice was heard, and we came in the hopes of sweet conversation. My tailless presumption, while waiting here, led me, indeed, to speak of thee. It is my hope that nothing was overheard."

Now the Jackal had spoken just to be listened to, for he knew flattery was the best way of getting things to eat, and the Mugger knew that the Jackal had spoken for this end, and the Jackal knew that the Mugger knew, and the Mugger knew that the Jackal knew that the Mugger knew, and so they were all very contented together.

The old brute pushed and panted and grunted up the bank, mumbling, "Respect the aged and infirm!" and all the time his little eyes burned like coals under the heavy, horny eyelids on the top of his triangular head, as he shoved his bloated barrel-body along between his crutched legs. Then he settled down, and, accustomed as the Jackal was to his ways, he could not help starting, for the hundredth time, when he saw how exactly the Mugger imitated a log adrift on the bar. He had even taken pains to lie at the exact angle a naturally stranded log would make with the water, having regard to the current of the season at the time and place. All this was only a matter of habit, of course, because the Mugger had come ashore for pleasure; but a crocodile is never quite full, and if the Jackal had been deceived by the likeness he would not have lived to philosophise over it.

"My child, I heard nothing," said the Mugger, shutting one eye. "The water was in my ears, and also I was faint with hunger. Since the railway bridge was built my people at my village have ceased to love me; and that is breaking my heart."

"Ah, shame!" said the Jackal. "So noble a heart, too! But men are all alike, to my mind."

"Nay, there are very great differences indeed," the Mugger answered gently. "Some are as lean as boat-poles. Others again are fat as young ja—dogs. Never would I causelessly revile men. They are of all fashions, but the long years have shown me that, one with another, they are very good. Men, women, and children—I have no fault to find with them. And remember, child, he who rebukes the World is rebuked by the World."

"Flattery is worse than an empty tin can in the belly. But that which we have just heard is wisdom," said the Adjutant, bringing down one foot.

"Consider, though, their ingratitude to this excellent one," began the Jackal tenderly.

"Nay, nay, not ingratitude!" the Mugger said. "They do not think for others; that is all. But I have noticed, lying at my station below the ford, that the stairs of the new bridge are cruelly hard to climb, both for old people and young children. The old, indeed, are not so worthy of consideration, but I am grieved—

I am truly grieved—on account of the fat children. Still, I think, in a little while, when the newness of the bridge has worn away, we shall see my people's bare brown legs bravely splashing through the ford as before. Then the old Mugger will be honoured again."

"But surely I saw marigold wreaths floating off the edge of the Ghaut only this noon," said the Adjutant. Marigold wreaths are a sign of reverence all India over.

"An error—an error. It was the wife of the sweet-meat-seller. She loses her eyesight year by year, and cannot tell a log from me—the Mugger of the Ghaut. I saw the mistake when she threw the garland, for I was lying at the very foot of the Ghaut, and had she taken another step I might have shown her some little difference. Yet she meant well, and we must consider the spirit of the offering."

"What good are marigold wreaths when one is on the rubbish-heap?" said the Jackal, hunting for fleas, but keeping one wary eye on his Protector of the Poor.

"True, but they have not yet begun to make the rubbish-heap that shall carry *me*. Five times have I seen the river draw back from the village and make new land at the foot of the street. Five times have I seen the village rebuilt on the banks, and I shall see it built yet five times more. I am no faithless, fish-hunting Gavial, I, at Kasi to-day and Prayag to-morrow, as the saying is, but the true and constant watcher of the ford. It is not for nothing, child, that the village bears my name, and 'he who watches long,' as the saying is, 'shall at last have his reward.'"

"*I* have watched long—very long—nearly all my life, and my reward has been bites and blows," said the Jackal.

"Ho! ho! ho!" roared the Adjutant.

"In August was the Jackal born;
The Rains fell in September;
'Now such a fearful flood as this,'
Says he, 'I can't remember!'"

There is one very unpleasant peculiarity about the Adjutant. At uncertain times he suffers from acute attacks of the fidgets or cramp in his legs, and though he is more virtuous to behold than any of the cranes, who are all immensely respectable, he flies off into wild, cripple-stilt war-dances, half opening his wings and bobbing his bald head up and down; while for reasons best known to himself he is very careful to time his worst attacks with his nastiest remarks. At the last word of his song he came to attention again, ten times adjutaunter than before.

The Jackal winced, though he was full three seasons old, but you cannot resent an insult from a person with a beak a yard long, and the power of driving it like a javelin. The Adjutant was a most notorious coward, but the Jackal was worse.

"We must live before we can learn," said the Mugger, "and there is this to say: Little jackals are very common, child, but such a mugger as I am is not common. For all that, I am not proud, since pride is destruction; but take notice, it is Fate, and against his Fate no one who swims or walks or runs should say anything at all. I am well contented with Fate. With good luck, a keen eye, and the custom of considering whether a creek or a backwater has an outlet to it ere you ascend, much may be done."

"Once I heard that even the Protector of the Poor made a mistake," said the Jackal viciously.

"True; but there my Fate helped me. It was before I had come to my full growth—before the last famine but three (by the Right and Left of Gunga, how full used the streams to be in those days!). Yes, I was young and unthinking, and when the flood came, who so pleased as I? A little made me very happy then. The village was deep in flood, and I swam above the Ghaut and went far inland, up to the rice-fields, and they were deep in good mud. I remember also a pair of bracelets (glass they were, and troubled me not a little) that I found that evening. Yes, glass bracelets; and, if my memory serves me well, a shoe. I should have shaken off both shoes, but I was hungry. I learned better later. Yes. And so I fed and rested me; but when I was ready to go to the river again the flood had fallen, and I walked through the mud of the main street. Who but I? Came out all my people, priests and women and children, and I looked upon them with benevolence. The mud is not a good place to fight in. Said a boatman, 'Get axes and kill him, for he is the Mugger of the ford.' 'Not so,' said the Brahmin. 'Look, he is driving the flood before him! He is the godling of the village. Then they threw many flowers at me, and by happy thought one led a goat across the road."

"How good—how very good is goat!" said the Jackal.

"Hairy—too hairy, and when found in the water more than likely to hide a cross-shaped hook. But that goat I accepted, and went down to the Ghaut in great honour. Later, my Fate sent me the boatman who had desired to cut off my tail with an axe. His boat grounded upon an old shoal which you would not remember."

"We are not *all* jackals here," said the Adjutant. "Was it the shoal made where the stone-boats sank in the year of the great drouth—a long shoal that lasted three floods?"

"There were two," said the Mugger; "an upper and a lower shoal."

"Ay, I forgot. A channel divided them, and later dried up again," said the Adjutant, who prided himself on his memory.

"On the lower shoal my well-wisher's craft grounded. He was sleeping in the bows, and, half awake, leaped over to his waist—no, it was no more than to his knees—to push off. His empty boat went on and touched again below the next reach, as the river ran then. I followed, because I knew men would come out to drag it ashore."

"And did they do so?" said the Jackal, a little awe-stricken. This was hunting on a scale that impressed him.

"There and lower down they did. I went no farther, but that gave me three in one day—well-fed *manjis* (boatmen) all, and, except in the case of the last (then I was careless), never a cry to warn those on the bank."

"Ah, noble sport! But what cleverness and great judgment it requires!" said the Jackal.

"Not cleverness, child, but only thought. A little thought in life is like salt upon rice, as the boatmen say, and I have thought deeply always. The Gavial, my cousin, the fish-eater, has told me how hard it is for him to follow his fish, and how one fish differs from the other, and how he must know them all, both together and apart. I say that is wisdom; but, on the other hand, my cousin, the Gavial, lives among his people. *My* people do not swim in companies, with their mouths out of the water, as Rewa does; nor do they constantly rise to the surface of the water, and turn over on their sides, like Mohoo and little Chapta; nor do they gather in shoals after flood, like Batchua and Chilwa."

"All are very good eating," said the Adjutant, clattering his beak.

"So my cousin says, and makes a great to-do over hunting them, but they do not climb the banks to escape his sharp nose. *My* people are otherwise. Their life is on the land, in the houses, among the cattle. I must know what they do, and what they are about to do; and, adding the tail to the trunk, as the saying is, I make up the whole elephant. Is there a green branch and an iron ring hanging over a doorway? The old Mugger knows that a boy has been born in that house, and must some day come down to the Ghaut to play. Is a maiden to be married? The old Mugger knows, for he sees the men carry gifts back and forth; and she, too, comes down to the Ghaut to bathe before her wedding, and—he is there. Has the river changed its channel, and made new land where there was only sand before? The Mugger knows."

"Now, of what use is that knowledge?" said the Jackal. "The river has shifted even in my little life." Indian rivers are nearly always moving about in their beds, and will shift, sometimes, as much as two or three miles in a season, drowning the fields on one bank, and spreading good silt on the other.

"There is no knowledge so useful," said the Mugger, "for new land means new quarrels. The Mugger knows. Oho! the Mugger knows. As soon as the water has drained off, he creeps up the little creeks that men think would not hide a dog, and there he waits. Presently comes a farmer saying he will plant cucumbers here, and melons there, in the new land that the river has given him. He feels the good mud with his bare toes. Anon comes another, saying he will put onions, and carrots, and sugar-cane in such and such places. They meet as boats adrift meet, and each rolls his eye at the other under the big blue turban. The old Mugger sees and hears. Each calls the other 'Brother,' and they go to mark out the boundaries of the new land. The Mugger hurries with them from point to point, shuffling very low through the mud. Now they begin to quarrel! Now they say hot words! Now they pull turbans! Now they lift up their *lathis* (clubs), and, at last, one falls backward into the mud, and the other runs away. When he comes back the dispute is settled, as the iron-bound bamboo of the loser witnesses. Yet they are not grateful to the Mugger. No, they cry 'Murder!' and their families fight with sticks, twenty a-side. My people are good people—upland Jats—Malwais of the Bêt. They do not give blows for sport, and, when the fight is done, the old Mugger waits far down the river, out of sight of the village, behind the *kikar*-scrub yonder. Then come they down, my broad-shouldered Jats—eight or nine together under the stars, bearing the dead man upon a bed. They are old men with gray beards, and voices as deep as mine. They light a little fire—ah! how well I know that fire!—and they drink tobacco, and they nod their heads together forward in a ring, or sideways toward the dead man upon the bank. They say the English Law will come with a rope for this matter, and that such a man's family will be ashamed, because such a man must be hanged in the great square of the Jail. Then say the friends of the dead, 'Let him hang!' and the talk is all to do over again—once, twice, twenty times in the long night. Then says one, at last, 'The fight was a fair fight. Let us take blood-money, a little more than is offered by the slayer, and we will say no more about it.' Then do they haggle over the blood-money, for the dead was a strong man, leaving many sons. Yet before *amratvela* (sunrise) they put the fire to him a

little, as the custom is, and the dead man comes to me,
and *he* says no more about it. Aha! my children, the
Mugger knows—the Mugger knows—and my Malwah
Jats are a good people!"

"They are too close—too narrow in the hand for my
crop," croaked the Adjutant. "They waste not the
polish on the cow's horn, as the saying is; and, again,
who can glean after a Malwai?"

"Ah, I—glean—*them*," said the Mugger.

"Now, in Calcutta of the South, in the old days,"
the Adjutant went on, "everything was thrown into
the streets, and we picked and chose. Those were
dainty seasons. But to-day they keep their streets as
clean as the outside of an egg, and my people fly away.
To be clean is one thing; to dust, sweep, and sprinkle
seven times a day wearies the very Gods themselves."

"There was a down-country jackal had it from a
brother, who told me, that in Calcutta of the South all
the jackals were as fat as otters in the Rains," said the
Jackal, his mouth watering at the bare thought of it.

"Ah, but the white-faces are there—the English,
and they bring dogs from somewhere down the river
in boats—big fat dogs—to keep those same jackals
lean," said the Adjutant.

"They are, then, as hard-hearted as these people? I
might have known. Neither earth, sky, nor water
shows charity to a jackal. I saw the tents of a white-
face last season, after the Rains, and I also took a new
yellow bridle to eat. The white-faces do not dress
their leather in the proper way. It made me very sick."

"That was better than my case," said the Adjutant.
"When I was in my third season, a young and a bold
bird, I went down to the river where the big boats
come in. The boats of the English are thrice as big as
this village."

"He has been as far as Delhi, and says all the people there walk on their heads," muttered the Jackal. The Mugger opened his left eye, and looked keenly at the Adjutant.

"It is true," the big bird insisted. "A liar only lies when he hopes to be believed. No one who had not seen those boats *could* believe this truth."

"*That* is more reasonable," said the Mugger. "And then?"

"From the insides of this boat they were taking out great pieces of white stuff, which, in a little while, turned to water. Much split off, and fell about on the shore, and the rest they swiftly put into a house with thick walls. But a boatman, who laughed, took a piece no larger than a small dog, and threw it to me. I—all my people—swallow without reflection, and that piece I swallowed as is our custom. Immediately I was afflicted with an excessive cold which, beginning in my crop, ran down to the extreme end of my toes, and deprived me even of speech, while the boatmen laughed at me. Never have I felt such cold. I danced in my grief and amazement till I could recover my breath, and then I danced and cried out against the falseness of this world; and the boatmen derided me till they fell down. The chief wonder of the matter, setting aside that marvellous coldness, was that there was nothing at all in my crop when I had finished my lamentings!"

The Adjutant had done his very best to describe his feelings after swallowing a seven-pound lump of Wenham Lake ice, off an American ice-ship, in the days before Calcutta made her ice by machinery; but as he did not know what ice was, and as the Mugger and the Jackal knew rather less, the tale missed fire.

"Anything," said the Mugger, shutting his left eye

again—"*anything* is possible that comes out of a boat thrice the size of Mugger-Ghaut. My village is not a small one."

There was a whistle overhead on the bridge, and the Delhi Mail slid across, all the carriages gleaming with light, and the shadows faithfully following along the river. It clanked away into the dark again; but the Mugger and the Jackal were so well used to it that they never turned their heads.

"Is there anything less wonderful than a boat thrice the size of Mugger-Ghaut?" said the bird, looking up.

"I saw that built, child. Stone by stone I saw the bridge-piers rise, and when the men fell off (they were wondrous sure-footed for the most part—but *when* they fell) I was ready. After the first pier was made they never thought to look down the stream for the body to burn. There, again, I saved much trouble. There was nothing strange in the building of the bridge," said the Mugger.

"But that which goes across, pulling the roofed carts! That is strange," the Adjutant repeated.

"It is, past any doubt, a new breed of bullock. Some day it will not be able to keep its foothold up yonder, and will fall as the men did. The old Mugger will then be ready."

The Jackal looked at the Adjutant, and the Adjutant looked at the Jackal. If there was one thing they were more certain of than another, it was that the engine was everything in the wide world except a bullock. The Jackal had watched it time and again from the aloe hedges by the side of the line, and the Adjutant had seen engines since the first locomotive ran in India. But the Mugger had only looked up at the thing from below, where the brass dome seemed rather like a bullock's hump.

"M—yes, a new kind of bullock," the Mugger repeated ponderously, to make himself quite sure in his own mind; and "Certainly it is a bullock," said the Jackal.

"And again it might be——" began the Mugger pettishly.

"Certainly—most certainly," said the Jackal, without waiting for the other to finish.

"What?" said the Mugger angrily, for he could feel that the others knew more than he did. "What might it be? *I* never finished my words. You said it was a bullock."

"It is anything the Protector of the Poor pleases. I am *his* servant—not the servant of the thing that crosses the river."

"Whatever it is, it is white-face work," said the Adjutant; "and for my own part, I would not lie out upon a place so near to it as this bar."

"You do not know the English as I do," said the Mugger. "There was a white-face here when the bridge was built, and he would take a boat in the evenings and shuffle with his feet on the bottom-boards, and whisper: 'Is he here? Is he there? Bring me my gun.' I could hear him before I could see him—each sound that he made—creaking and puffing and rattling his gun, up and down the river. As surely as I had picked up one of his workmen, and thus saved great expense in wood for the burning, so surely would he come down to the Ghaut, and shout in a loud voice that he would hunt me, and rid the river of me—the Mugger of Mugger-Ghaut! *Me!* Children, I have swum under the bottom of his boat for hour after hour, and heard him fire his gun at logs; and when I was well sure he was wearied, I have risen by his side and snapped my jaws in his face. When the bridge was finished he went away. All the English hunt in that fashion, except when they are hunted."

"Who hunts the white-faces?" yapped the Jackal excitedly.

"No one now, but I have hunted them in my time."

"I remember a little of that Hunting. I was young then," said the Adjutant, clattering his beak significantly.

"I was well established here. My village was being builded for the third time, as I remember, when my cousin, the Gavial, brought me word of rich waters above Benares. At first I would not go, for my cousin, who is a fish-eater, does not always know the good from the bad; but I heard my people talking in the evenings, and what they said made me certain."

"And what did they say?" the Jackal asked.

"They said enough to make me, the Mugger of Mugger-Ghaut, leave water and take to my feet. I went by night, using the littlest streams as they served me; but it was the beginning of the hot weather, and all streams were low. I crossed dusty roads; I went through tall grass; I climbed hills in the moonlight. Even rocks did I climb, children—consider this well. I crossed the tail of Sirhind, the waterless, before I could find the set of the little rivers that flow Gunga-ward. I was a month's journey from my own people and the river that I knew. That was very marvellous!"

"What food on the way?" said the Jackal, who kept his soul in his little stomach, and was not a bit impressed by the Mugger's land travels.

"That which I could find—*cousin*," said the Mugger slowly, dragging each word.

Now you do not call a man a cousin in India unless you think you can establish some kind of blood-relationship, and as it is only in old fairy-tales that the

Mugger ever marries a jackal, the Jackal knew for
what reason he had been suddenly lifted into the Mugger's family circle. If they had been alone he would not
have cared, but the Adjutant's eyes twinkled with
mirth at the ugly jest.

"Assuredly, Father, I might have known," said the
Jackal. A mugger does not care to be called a father
of jackals, and the Mugger of Mugger-Ghaut said as
much—and a great deal more which there is no use in
repeating here.

"The Protector of the Poor has claimed kinship.
How can I remember the precise degree? Moreover,
we eat the same food. He has said it," was the Jackal's
reply.

That made matters rather worse, for what the Jackal
hinted at was that the Mugger must have eaten his
food on that land-march fresh and fresh every day,
instead of keeping it by him till it was in a fit and
proper condition, as every self-respecting mugger
and most wild beasts do when they can. Indeed, one
of the worst terms of contempt along the River-bed
is "eater of fresh meat." It is nearly as bad as calling
a man a cannibal.

"That food was eaten thirty seasons ago," said the
Adjutant quietly. "If we talk for thirty seasons more
it will never come back. Tell us, now, what happened
when the good waters were reached after thy most
wonderful land journey. If we listened to the howling
of every jackal the business of the town would stop,
as the saying is."

The Mugger must have been grateful for the inter-
ruption, because he went on, with a rush:

"By the Right and Left of Gunga! when I came
there never did I see such waters!"

"Were they better, then, than the big flood of last
season?" said the Jackal.

"Better! That flood was no more than comes every five years—a handful of drowned strangers, some chickens, and a dead bullock in muddy water with cross-currents. But the season I think of, the river was low, smooth, and even, and, as the Gavial had warned me, the dead English came down, touching each other. I got my girth in that season—my girth and my depth. From Agra, by Etawah and the broad waters by Allahabad——"

"Oh, the eddy that set under the walls of the fort at Allahabad!" said the Adjutant. "They came in there like widgeon to the reeds, and round and round they swung—thus!"

He went off into his horrible dance again, while the Jackal looked on enviously. He naturally could not remember the terrible year of the Mutiny they were talking about. The Mugger continued:

"Yes, by Allahabad one lay still in the slack-water and let twenty go by to pick one; and, above all, the English were not cumbered with jewellery and nose-rings and anklets as my women are nowadays. To delight in ornaments is to end with a rope for necklace, as the saying is. All the muggers of all the rivers grew fat then, but it was my Fate to be fatter than them all. The news was that the English were being hunted into the rivers, and by the Right and Left of Gunga! we believed it was true. So far as I went south I believed it to be true; and I went down-stream beyond Monghyr and the tombs that look over the river."

"I know that place," said the Adjutant. "Since those days Monghyr is a lost city. Very few live there now."

"Thereafter I worked up-stream very slowly and lazily, and a little above Monghyr there came down a boatful of white-faces—alive! They were, as I remember, women, lying under a cloth spread over sticks, and crying aloud. There was never a gun fired at us,

the watchers of the fords in those days. All the guns
were busy elsewhere. We could hear them day and
night inland, coming and going as the wind shifted. I
rose up full before the boat, because I had never seen
white-faces alive, though I knew them well—otherwise. A naked white child kneeled by the side of the
boat, and, stooping over, must needs try to trail his
hands in the river. It is a pretty thing to see how a child
loves running water. I had fed that day, but there was
yet a little unfilled space within me. Still, it was for
sport and not for food that I rose at the child's hands.
They were so clear a mark that I did not even look
when I closed; but they were so small that though my
jaws rang true—I am sure of that—the child drew them
up swiftly, unhurt. They must have passed between
tooth and tooth—those small white hands. I should have
caught him cross-wise at the elbows; but, as I said, it
was only for sport and desire to see new things that I
rose at all. They cried out one after another in the
boat, and presently I rose again to watch them. The
boat was too heavy to push over. They were only
women, but he who trusts a woman will walk on duck-
weed in a pool, as the saying is: and by the Right and
Left of Gunga, that is truth!"

"Once a woman gave me some dried skin from a
fish," said the Jackal. "I had hoped to get her baby,
but horse-food is better than the kick of a horse, as
the saying is. What did thy woman do?"

"She fired at me with a short gun of a kind I have
never seen before or since. Five times, one after another" (the Mugger must have met with an old-
fashioned revolver); "and I stayed open-mouthed and
gaping, my head in the smoke. Never did I see such a
thing. Five times, as swiftly as I wave my tail—thus!"

The Jackal, who had been growing more and more

interested in the story, had just time to leap back as the huge tail swung by like a scythe.

"Not before the fifth shot," said the Mugger, as though he had never dreamed of stunning one of his listeners—"not before the fifth shot did I sink, and I rose in time to hear a boatman telling all those white women that I was most certainly dead. One bullet had gone under a neck-plate of mine. I know not if it is there still, for the reason I cannot turn my head. Look and see, child. It will show that my tale is true."

"I?" said the Jackal. "Shall an eater of old shoes, a bone-cracker, presume to doubt the word of the Envy of the River? May my tail be bitten off by blind puppies if the shadow of such a thought had crossed my humble mind! The Protector of the Poor has condescended to inform me, his slave, that once in his life he has been wounded by a woman. That is sufficient, and I will tell the tale to all my children, asking for no proof."

"Over-much civility is sometimes no better than over-much discourtesy, for, as the saying is, one can choke a guest with curds. I do *not* desire that any children of thine should know that the Mugger of Mugger-Ghaut took his only wound from a woman. They will have much else to think of if they get their meat as miserably as does their father."

"It is forgotten long ago! It was never said! There never was a white woman! There was no boat! Nothing whatever happened at all."

The Jackal waved his brush to show how completely everything was wiped out of his memory, and sat down with an air.

"Indeed, very many things happened," said the Mugger, beaten in his second attempt that night to get the better of his friend. (Neither bore malice, how-

ever. Eat and be eaten was fair law along the river, and
the Jackal came in for his share of plunder when the
Mugger had finished a meal.) "I left that boat and
went up-stream, and, when I had reached Arrah and
the back-waters behind it, there were no more dead
English. The river was empty for a while. Then came
one or two dead, in red coats, not English, but of one
kind all—Hindus and Purbeeahs—then five and six
abreast, and at last, from Arrah to the North beyond
Agra, it was as though whole villages had walked into
the water. They came out of little creeks one after another, as the logs come down in the Rains. When the
river rose they rose also in companies from the shoals
they had rested upon; and the falling flood dragged
them with it across the fields and through the Jungle
by the long hair. All night, too, going North, I heard
the guns, and by day the shod feet of men crossing
fords, and that noise which a heavy cart-wheel makes
on sand under water; and every ripple brought more
dead. At last even I was afraid, for I said: 'If this thing
happen to men, how shall the Mugger of Mugger-
Ghaut escape?' There were boats, too, that came up
behind me without sails, burning continually, as the
cotton-boats sometimes burn, but never sinking."

"Ah!" said the Adjutant. "Boats like those come to
Calcutta of the South. They are tall and black, they
beat up the water behind them with a tail, and
they——"

"Are thrice as big as my village. *My* boats were low
and white; they beat up the water on either side of
them, and were no larger than the boats of one who
speaks truth should be. They made me very afraid, and
I left water and went back to this my river, hiding by
day and walking by night, when I could not find little
streams to help me. I came to my village again, but I

did not hope to see any of my people there. Yet they were ploughing and sowing and reaping, and going to and fro in their fields, as quietly as their own cattle."

"Was there still good food in the river?" said the Jackal.

"More than I had any desire for. Even I—and I do not eat mud—even I was tired, and, as I remember, a little frightened of this constant coming down of the silent ones. I heard my people say in my village that all the English were dead; but those that came, face down, with the current were *not* English, as my people saw. Then my people said that it was best to say nothing at all, but to pay the tax and plough the land. After a long time the river cleared, and those that came down it had been clearly drowned by the floods, as I could well see; and though it was not so easy then to get food, I was heartily glad of it. A little killing here and there is no bad thing—but even the Mugger is sometimes satisfied, as the saying is."

"Marvellous! Most truly marvellous!" said the Jackal. "I am become fat through merely hearing about so much good eating. And afterward what, if it be permitted to ask, did the Protector of the Poor do?"

"I said to myself—and by the Right and Left of Gunga! I locked my jaws on that vow—I said I would never go roving any more. So I lived by the Ghaut, very close to my own people, and I watched over them year after year; and they loved me so much that they threw marigold wreaths at my head whenever they saw it lift. Yes, and my Fate has been very kind to me, and the river is good enough to respect my poor and infirm presence; only——"

"No one is all happy from his beak to his tail," said the Adjutant sympathetically. "What does the Mugger of Mugger-Ghaut need more?"

"That little white child which I did not get," said the Mugger, with a deep sigh. "He was very small, but I have not forgotten. I am old now, but before I die it is my desire to try one new thing. It is true they are a heavy-footed, noisy, and foolish people, and the sport would be small, but I remember the old days above Benares, and, if the child lives, he will remember still. It may be he goes up and down the bank of some river, telling how he once passed his hands between the teeth of the Mugger of Mugger-Ghaut, and lived to make a tale of it. My Fate has been very kind, but that plagues me sometimes in my dreams—the thought of the little white child in the bows of that boat." He yawned, and closed his jaws. "And now I will rest and think. Keep silent, my children, and respect the aged."

He turned stiffly, and shuffled to the top of the sandbar, while the Jackal drew back with the Adjutant to the shelter of a tree stranded on the end nearest the railway bridge.

"That was a pleasant and profitable life," he grinned, looking up inquiringly at the bird who towered above him. "And not once, mark you, did he think fit to tell me where a morsel might have been left along the banks. Yet I have told *him* a hundred times of good things wallowing down-stream. How true is the saying, 'All the world forgets the Jackal and the Barber when the news has been told!' Now he is going to sleep! *Arrh!*"

"How can a Jackal hunt with a Mugger?" said the Adjutant coolly. "Big thief and little thief; it is easy to say who gets the pickings."

The Jackal turned, whining impatiently, and was going to curl himself up under the tree-trunk, when suddenly he cowered, and looked up through the draggled branches at the bridge almost above his head.

"What now?" said the Adjutant, opening his wings uneasily.

"Wait till we see. The wind blows from us to them, but they are not looking for us—those two men."

"Men, is it? My office protects me. All India knows I am holy." The Adjutant, being a first-class scavenger, is allowed to go where he pleases, and so this one never flinched.

"I am not worth a blow from anything better than an old shoe," said the Jackal, and listened again. "Hark to that footfall!" he went on. "That was no country leather, but the shod foot of a white-face. Listen again! Iron hits iron up there! It is a gun! Friend, those heavy-footed, foolish English are coming to speak with the Mugger."

"Warn him, then. He was called Protector of the Poor by some one not unlike a starving Jackal but a little time ago."

"Let my cousin protect his own hide. He has told me again and again there is nothing to fear from the white-faces. They must be white-faces. Not a villager of Mugger-Ghaut would dare to come after him. See,

I said it was a gun! Now, with good luck, we shall feed before daylight. He cannot hear well out of water, and—this time it is not a woman!"

A shiny barrel glittered for a minute in the moonlight on the girders. The Mugger was lying on the sand-bar as still as his own shadow, his fore-feet spread out a little, his head dropped between them, snoring like a—mugger.

A voice on the bridge whispered: "It's an odd shot —straight down almost—but as safe as houses. Better try behind the neck. Golly! what a brute! The villagers will be wild if he's shot, though. He's the *deota* [godling] of these parts."

"Don't care a rap," another voice answered; "he took about fifteen of my best coolies while the bridge was building, and it's time he was put a stop to. I've been after him in a boat for weeks. Stand by with the Martini as soon as I've given him both barrels of this."

"Mind the kick, then. A double four-bore's no joke."

"That's for him to decide. Here goes!"

There was a roar like the sound of a small cannon (the biggest sort of elephant-rifle is not very different from some artillery), and a double streak of flame, followed by the stinging crack of a Martini, whose long bullet makes nothing of a crocodile's plates. But the explosive bullets did the work. One of them struck just behind the Mugger's neck, a hand's-breadth to the left of the backbone, while the other burst a little lower down, at the beginning of the tail. In ninety-nine cases out of a hundred a mortally-wounded crocodile can scramble to deep water and get away; but the Mugger of Mugger-Ghaut was literally broken into three pieces. He hardly moved his head before the life went out of him, and he lay as flat as the Jackal.

". . . HE CREEPS UP THE LITTLE CREEKS THAT MEN THINK WOULD NOT
HIDE A DOG . . ." (*page 91*)

"Thunder and lightning! Lightning and thunder!" said that miserable little beast. "Has the thing that pulls the covered carts over the bridge tumbled at last?"

"It is no more than a gun," said the Adjutant, though his very tail-feathers quivered. "Nothing more than a gun. He is certainly dead. Here come the white-faces."

The two Englishmen had hurried down from the bridge and across to the sand-bar, where they stood admiring the length of the Mugger. Then a native with an axe cut off the big head, and four men dragged it across the spit.

"The last time that I had my hand in a Mugger's mouth," said one of the Englishmen, stooping down (he was the man who had built the bridge), "it was when I was about five years old—coming down the river by boat to Monghyr. I was a Mutiny baby, as they called it. Poor mother was in the boat, too, and she often told me how she fired dad's old pistol at the beast's head."

"Well, you've certainly had your revenge on the chief of the clan—even if the gun has made your nose bleed. Hi, you boatmen! Haul that head up the bank, and we'll boil it for the skull. The skin's too knocked about to keep. Come along to bed now. This was worth sitting up all night for, wasn't it?"

Curiously enough, the Jackal and the Adjutant made the very same remark not three minutes after the men had left.

A RIPPLE SONG

Once a ripple came to land
    In the golden sunset burning—
Lapped against a maiden's hand,
    By the ford returning.

Dainty foot and gentle breast—
Here, across, be glad and rest.
"Maiden, wait," the ripple saith;
"Wait awhile, for I am Death!"

"Where my lover calls I go—
    Shame it were to treat him coldly—
'Twas a fish that circled so,
    Turning over boldly."

Dainty foot and tender heart,
Wait the loaded ferry-cart.
"Wait, ah, wait!" the ripple saith;
"Maiden, wait, for I am Death!"

"When my lover calls I haste—
    Dame Disdain was never wedded!"
Ripple-ripple round her waist,
    Clear the current eddied.

Foolish heart and faithful hand,
Little feet that touched no land.
Far away the ripple sped,
Ripple—ripple—running red!

QUIQUERN

QUIQUERN

The People of the Eastern Ice, they are melting like
*   the snow—*
They beg for coffee and sugar; they go where the
*   white men go.*
The People of the Western Ice, they learn to steal and
*   fight;*
They sell their furs to the trading-post: they sell their
*   souls to the white.*
The People of the Southern Ice, they trade with the
*   whaler's crew;*
Their women have many ribbons, but their tents are
*   torn and few.*
But the People of the Elder Ice, beyond the white
*   man's ken—*
Their spears are made of the narwhal-horn, and they
*   are the last of the Men!*

                                Translation

"HE HAS opened his eyes. Look!"

"Put him in the skin again. He will be a strong dog. On the fourth month we will name him."

"For whom?" said Amoraq.

Kadlu's eye rolled round the skin-lined snow-house till it fell on fourteen-year-old Kotuko sitting on the

sleeping-bench, making a button out of walrus ivory.
"Name him for me," said Kotuko, with a grin. "I shall
need him one day."

Kadlu grinned back till his eyes were almost buried
in the fat of his flat cheeks, and nodded to Amoraq,
while the puppy's fierce mother whined to see her
baby wriggling far out of reach in the little sealskin
pouch hung above the warmth of the blubber-lamp.
Kotuko went on with his carving, and Kadlu threw a
rolled bundle of leather dog-harnesses into a tiny little
room that opened from one side of the house, slipped
off his heavy deerskin hunting-suit, put it into a whale-
bone-net that hung above another lamp, and dropped
down on the sleeping-bench to whittle at a piece of
frozen seal-meat till Amoraq, his wife, should bring
the regular dinner of boiled meat and blood-soup. He
had been out since early dawn at the seal-holes, eight
miles away, and had come home with three big seal.
Half-way down the long, low snow passage or tunnel
that led to the inner door of the house you could hear
snappings and yelpings, as the dogs of his sleigh-team,
released from the day's work, scuffled for warm places.

When the yelpings grew too loud Kotuko lazily
rolled off the sleeping-bench, and picked up a whip
with an eighteen-inch handle of springy whalebone,
and twenty-five feet of heavy, plaited thong. He dived
into the passage, where it sounded as though all the
dogs were eating him alive; but that was no more than
their regular grace before meals. When he crawled
out at the far end, half a dozen furry heads followed
him with their eyes as he went to a sort of gallows of
whale-jawbones, from which the dog's meat was
hung; split off the frozen stuff in big lumps with a
broad-headed spear; and stood, his whip in one hand
and the meat in the other. Each beast was called by

name, the weakest first, and woe betide any dog that moved out of his turn; for the tapering lash would shoot out like thonged lightning, and flick away an inch or so of hair and hide. Each beast growled, snapped, choked once over his portion, and hurried back to the protection of the passage, while the boy stood upon the snow under the blazing Northern Lights and dealt out justice. The last to be served was the big black leader of the team, who kept order when the dogs were harnessed; and to him Kotuko gave a double allowance of meat as well as an extra crack of the whip.

"Ah!" said Kotuko, coiling up the lash, "I have a little one over the lamp that will make a great many howlings. *Sarpok!* Get in!"

He crawled back over the huddled dogs, dusted the dry snow from his furs with the whalebone beater that Amoraq kept by the door, tapped the skin-lined roof of the house to shake off any icicles that might have fallen from the dome of snow above, and curled up on the bench. The dogs in the passage snored and whined in their sleep, the boy-baby in Amoraq's deep fur hood kicked and choked and gurgled, and the mother of the newly-named puppy lay at Kotuko's side, her eyes fixed on the bundle of sealskin, warm and safe above the broad yellow flame of the lamp.

And all this happened far away to the north, beyond Labrador, beyond Hudson's Strait, where the great tides heave the ice about, north of Melville Peninsula —north even of the narrow Fury and Hecla Straits— on the north shore of Baffin Land, where Bylot's Island stands above the ice of Lancaster Sound like a pudding-bowl wrong side up. North of Lancaster Sound there is little we know anything about, except North Devon and Ellesmere Land; but even there live a few scattered people, next door, as it were, to the very Pole.

Kadlu was an Inuit,—what you call an Esquimau,—and his tribe, some thirty persons all told, belong to the Tununirmiut—"the country lying at the back of something." In the maps that desolate coast is written Navy Board Inlet, but the Inuit name is best, because the

country lies at the very back of everything in the world. For nine months of the year there is only ice and snow, and gale after gale, with a cold that no one can realise who has never seen the thermometer even at zero. For six months of those nine it is dark; and that is what makes it so horrible. In the three months of the summer it only freezes every other day and every night, and then the snow begins to weep off on the southerly slopes, and a few ground-willows put out their woolly buds, a tiny stonecrop or so makes believe to blossom, beaches of fine gravel and rounded stones run down to the open sea, and polished boulders and streaked rocks lift up above the granulated snow. But all that is gone in a few weeks, and the wild winter locks down again on the land; while at sea the ice tears up and down the offing, jamming and ramming, and splitting and hitting, and pounding and grounding, till it all freezes together, ten feet thick, from the land outward to deep water.

In the winter Kadlu would follow the seal to the edge of this land-ice, and spear them as they came up to breathe at their blow-holes. The seal must have open water to live and catch fish in, and in the deep of winter the ice would sometimes run eighty miles without a break from the nearest shore. In the spring he and his people retreated from the floes to the rocky mainland, where they put up tents of skins, and snared the sea-birds, or speared the young seal basking on the beaches. Later, they would go south into Baffin Land after the reindeer, and to get their year's store of salmon from the hundreds of streams and lakes of the interior; coming back north in September or October for the musk-ox hunting and the regular winter sealery. This travelling was done with dog-sleighs, twenty and thirty miles a day, or sometimes down the coast in big skin "woman-boats," when the dogs and the babies lay among the feet of the rowers, and the women sang songs as they glided from cape to cape over the glassy, cold waters. All the luxuries that the Tununirmiut knew came from the south—driftwood for sleigh-runners, rod-iron for harpoon-tips, steel knives, tin kettles that cooked food much better than the old soap-stone affairs, flint and steel, and even matches, as well as coloured ribbons for the women's hair, little cheap mirrors, and red cloth for the edging of deerskin dress-packets. Kadlu traded the rich, creamy, twisted narwhal horn and musk-ox teeth (these are just as valuable as pearls) to the Southern Inuit, and they, in turn, traded with the whalers and the missionary-posts of Exeter and Cumberland Sounds; and so the chain went on, till a kettle picked up by a ship's cook in the Bhendy Bazaar might end its days over a blubber-lamp somewhere on the cool side of the Arctic Circle.

Kadlu, being a good hunter, was rich in iron harpoons, snow-knives, bird-darts, and all the other things that make life easy up there in the great cold; and he was the head of his tribe, or, as they say, "the man who knows all about it by practice." This did not give him any authority, except now and then he could advise his friends to change their hunting-grounds; but Kotuko used it to domineer a little, in the lazy, fat Inuit fashion, over the other boys, when they came out at night to play ball in the moonlight, or to sing the Child's Song to the Aurora Borealis.

But at fourteen an Inuit feels himself a man, and Kotuko was tired of making snares for wild-fowl and kit-foxes, and most tired of all of helping the women to chew seal- and deer-skins (that supples them as nothing else can) the long day through, while the men were out hunting. He wanted to go into the *quaggi*, the Singing-House, when the hunters gathered there for their mysteries, and the *angekok*, the sorcerer, frightened them into the most delightful fits after the lamps were put out, and you could hear the Spirit of the Reindeer stamping on the roof; and when a spear was thrust out into the open black night it came back covered with hot blood. He wanted to throw his big boots into the net with the tired air of the head of a family, and to gamble with the hunters when they dropped in of an evening and played a sort of home-made roulette with a tin pot and a nail. There were hundreds of things that he wanted to do, but the grown men laughed at him and said, "Wait till you have been in the buckle, Kotuko. Hunting is not *all* catching."

Now that his father had named a puppy for him, things looked brighter. An Inuit does not waste a good dog on his son till the boy knows something of dog-driving; and Kotuko was more than sure that he knew more than everything.

If the puppy had not had an iron constitution he would have died from over-stuffing and over-handling. Kotuko made him a tiny harness with a trace to it, and hauled him all over the house-floor, shouting: "Aua! Ja aua!" (Go to the right). "Choiachoi! Ja choiachoi!" (Go to the left). "Ohaha!" (Stop). The puppy did not like it at all, but being fished for in this way was pure happiness beside being put to the sleigh for the first time. He just sat down on the snow, and played with the seal-hide trace that ran from his harness to the *pitu*, the big thong in the bows of the sleigh. Then the team started, and the puppy found the heavy ten-foot sleigh running up his back, and dragging him along the snow, while Kotuko laughed till the tears ran down his face. There followed days and days of the cruel whip that hisses like the wind over ice, and his companions all bit him because he did not know his work, and the harness chafed him, and he was not allowed to sleep with Kotuko any more, but had to take the coldest place in the passage. It was a sad time for the puppy.

The boy learned, too, as fast as the dog; though a dog-sleigh is a heart-breaking thing to manage. Each beast is harnessed, the weakest nearest to the driver, by his own separate trace, which runs under his left fore-leg to the main thong, where it is fastened by a sort of button and loop which can be slipped by a turn of the

wrist, thus freeing one dog at a time. This is very
necessary, because young dogs often get the trace between their hind legs, where it cuts to the bone. And
they one and all *will* go visiting their friends as they
run, jumping in and out among the traces. Then they
fight, and the result is more mixed than a wet fishing-
line next morning. A great deal of trouble can be
avoided by scientific use of the whip. Every Inuit boy
prides himself as being a master of the long lash; but it
is easy to flick at a mark on the ground, and difficult
to lean forward and catch a shirking dog just behind
the shoulders when the sleigh is going at full speed. If
you call one dog's name for "visiting," and acciden-
tally lash another, the two will fight it out at once, and
stop all the others. Again, if you travel with a com-
panion and begin to talk, or by yourself and sing, the
dogs will halt, turn round, and sit down to hear what
you have to say. Kotuko was run away from once or
twice through forgetting to block the sleigh when he
stopped; and he broke many lashings, and ruined a few
thongs before he could be trusted with a full team of
eight and the light sleigh. Then he felt himself a person of consequence, and on smooth, black ice, with a
bold heart and a quick elbow, he smoked along over
the levels as fast as a pack in full cry. He would go ten
miles to the seal-holes, and when he was on the hunting-grounds he would twitch a trace loose from the
pitu, and free the big black leader, who was the clever-
est dog in the team. As soon as the dog had scented a
breathing-hole, Kotuko would reverse the sleigh, driving a couple of sawed-off antlers, that stuck up like
perambulator-handles from the back-rest, deep into
the snow, so that the team could not get away. Then
he would crawl forward inch by inch, and wait till
the seal came up to breathe. Then he would stab down

swiftly with his spear and running-line, and presently would haul his seal up to the lip of the ice, while the black leader came up and helped to pull the carcass across the ice to the sleigh. That was the time when the harnessed dogs yelled and foamed with excitement, and Kotuko laid the long lash like a red-hot bar across all their faces, till the carcass froze stiff. Going home was the heavy work. The loaded sleigh had to be humoured among the rough ice, and the dogs sat down and looked hungrily at the seal instead of pulling. At last they would strike the well-worn sleigh-road to the village, and toodle-kiyi along the ringing ice, heads down and tails up, while Kotuko struck up the "Angutivaun tai-na tau-na-ne taina" (The Song of the Returning Hunter), and voices hailed him from house to house under all that dim, star-litten sky.

When Kotuko the dog came to his full growth he enjoyed himself too. He fought his way up the team steadily, fight after fight, till one fine evening, over their food, he tackled the big, black leader (Kotuko the boy saw fair play), and made second dog of him, as they say. So he was promoted to the long thong of the leading dog, running five feet in advance of all the others: it was his bounden duty to stop all fighting, in harness or out of it, and he wore a collar of copper wire, very thick and heavy. On special occasions he was fed with cooked food inside the house, and sometimes was allowed to sleep on the bench with Kotuko. He was a good seal-dog, and would keep a musk-ox at bay by running round him and snapping at his heels. He would even—and this for a sleigh-dog is the last proof of bravery—he would even stand up to the gaunt Arctic wolf, whom all dogs of the North, as a rule, fear beyond anything that walks the snow. He and his master—they did not count the team of ordinary dogs as company—hunted together, day after day and night after night, fur-wrapped boy and savage, long-haired, narrow-eyed, white-fanged, yellow brute. All an Inuit has to do is to get food and skins for himself and his family. The women-folk make the skins into clothing, and occasionally help in trapping small game; but the bulk of the food—and they eat enormously—must be found by the men. If the supply fails there is no one up there to buy or beg or borrow from. The people must die.

An Inuit does not think of these chances till he is forced to. Kadlu, Kotuko, Amoraq, and the boy-baby who kicked about in Amoraq's fur hood and chewed pieces of blubber all day, were as happy together as any family in the world. They came of a very gentle race—an Inuit seldom loses his temper, and almost never strikes a child—who did not know exactly what telling a real lie meant, still less how to steal. They were content to spear their living out of the heart of the bitter, hopeless cold; to smile oily smiles, and tell queer ghost and fairy tales of evenings, and eat till they could eat no more, and sing the endless woman's song: "Amna aya, aya amna, ah! ah!" through the long lamp-lighted days as they mended their clothes and their hunting-gear.

But one terrible winter everything betrayed them. The Tununirmiut returned from the yearly salmon-fishing, and made their houses on the early ice to the north of Bylot's Island, ready to go after the seal as soon as the sea froze. But it was an early and savage autumn. All through September there were continuous gales that broke up the smooth seal-ice when it was only four or five feet thick, and forced it inland, and piled a great barrier, some twenty miles broad, of lumped and ragged and needly ice, over which it was

impossible to draw the dog-sleighs. The edge of the
floe off which the seal were used to fish in winter lay
perhaps twenty miles beyond this barrier, and out of
reach of the Tununirmiut. Even so, they might have
managed to scrape through the winter on their stock of
frozen salmon and stored blubber, and what the traps
gave them, but in December one of their hunters came
across a *tupik* (a skin-tent) of three women and a girl
nearly dead, whose men had come down from the far
North and been crushed in their little skin hunting-
boats while they were out after the long-horned narwhal. Kadlu, of course, could only distribute the
women among the huts of the winter village, for no
Inuit dare refuse a meal to a stranger. He never knows
when his own turn may come to beg. Amoraq took the
girl, who was about fourteen, into her own house as
a sort of servant. From the cut of her sharp-pointed
hood, and the long diamond pattern of her white deerskin leggings, they supposed she came from Ellesmere
Land. She had never seen tin cooking-pots or wooden-
shod sleighs before; but Kotuko the boy and Kotuko
the dog were rather fond of her.

Then all the foxes went south, and even the wolver-
ine, that growling, blunt-headed little thief of the
snow, did not take the trouble to follow the line of
empty traps that Kotuko set. The tribe lost a couple of
their best hunters, who were badly crippled in a fight
with a musk-ox, and this threw more work on the
others. Kotuko went out, day after day, with a light
hunting-sleigh and six or seven of the strongest dogs,
looking till his eyes ached for some patch of clear ice
where a seal might perhaps have scratched a breathing-hole. Kotuko the dog ranged far and wide, and in
the dead stillness of the ice-fields Kotuko the boy
could hear his half-choked whine of excitement, above

a seal-hole three miles away, as plainly as though he were at his elbow. When the dog found a hole the boy would build himself a little, low snow wall to keep off the worst of the bitter wind, and there he would wait ten, twelve, twenty hours for the seal to come up to breathe, his eyes glued to the tiny mark he had made above the hole to guide the downward thrust of his harpoon, a little seal-skin mat under his feet, and his legs tied together in the *tutareang* (the buckle that the old hunters had talked about). This helps to keep a man's legs from twitching as he waits and waits and waits for the quick-eared seal to rise. Though there is no excitement in it, you can easily believe that the sitting still in the buckle with the thermometer perhaps forty degrees below zero is the hardest work an Inuit knows. When a seal was caught, Kotuko the dog would bound forward, his trace trailing behind him, and help to pull the body to the sleigh, where the tired and hungry dogs lay sullenly under the lee of the broken ice.

A seal did not go very far, for each mouth in the little village had a right to be filled, and neither bone, hide, nor sinew was wasted. The dogs' meat was taken for human use, and Amoraq fed the team with pieces of old summer skin-tents raked out from under the sleeping-bench, and they howled and howled again, and waked to howl hungrily. One could tell by the soap-stone lamps in the huts that famine was near. In good seasons, when blubber was plentiful, the light in the boat-shaped lamps would be two feet high—cheerful, oily, and yellow. Now it was a bare six inches: Amoraq carefully pricked down the moss wick, when an unwatched flame brightened for a moment, and the eyes of all the family followed her hand. The horror of famine up there in the great cold is not so much dying, as dying in the dark. All the Inuit dread the dark that presses on them without a break for six months in each year; and when the lamps are low in the houses the minds of people begin to be shaken and confused.

But worse was to come.

The underfed dogs snapped and growled in the passages, glaring at the cold stars, and snuffing into the bitter wind, night after night. When they stopped howling the silence fell down again as solid and as heavy as a snowdrift against a door, and men could hear the beating of their blood in the thin passages of the ear, and the thumping of their own hearts, that sounded as loud as the noise of sorcerers' drums beaten across the snow. One night Kotuko the dog, who had been unusually sullen in harness, leaped up and pushed his head against Kotuko's knee. Kotuko patted him, but the dog still pushed blindly forward, fawning. Then Kadlu waked, and gripped the heavy wolf-like head, and stared into the glassy eyes. The dog whimpered and shivered between Kadlu's knees. The hair rose about his neck, and he growled as though a stranger were at the door; then he barked joyously, and rolled on the ground, and bit at Kotuko's boot like a puppy.

"What is it?" said Kotuko; for he was beginning to be afraid.

"The sickness," Kadlu answered. "It is the dog-sickness." Kotuko the dog lifted his nose and howled and howled again.

"I have not seen this before. What will he do?" said Kotuko.

Kadlu shrugged one shoulder a little, and crossed the hut for his short stabbing-harpoon. The big dog looked at him, howled again, and slunk away down the

passage, while the other dogs drew aside right and left
to give him ample room. When he was out on the snow
he barked furiously, as though on the trail of a
musk-ox, and, barking and leaping and frisking, passed
out of sight. His trouble was not hydrophobia, but
simple, plain madness. The cold and the hunger, and,
above all, the dark, had turned his head; and when the
terrible dog-sickness once shows itself in a team, it
spreads like wild-fire. Next hunting-day another dog
sickened, and was killed then and there by Kotuko as
he bit and struggled among the traces. Then the black
second dog, who had been the leader in the old days,
suddenly gave tongue on an imaginary reindeer-track,
and when they slipped him from the *pitu* he flew at
the throat of an ice-cliff, and ran away as his leader
had done, his harness on his back. After that no one
would take the dogs out again. They needed them for
something else, and the dogs knew it; and though they
were tied down and fed by hand, their eyes were full
of despair and fear. To make things worse, the old
women began to tell ghost-tales, and to say that they
had met the spirits of the dead hunters lost that autumn,
who prophesied all sorts of horrible things.

Kotuko grieved more for the loss of his dog than
anything else; for though an Inuit eats enormously he
also knows how to starve. But the hunger, the darkness,
the cold, and the exposure told on his strength, and he
began to hear voices inside his head, and to see people
who were not there, out of the tail of his eye. One
night—he had unbuckled himself after ten hours' waiting above a "blind" seal-hole, and was staggering back
to the village faint and dizzy—he halted to lean his back
against a boulder which happened to be supported like
a rocking-stone on a single jutting point of ice. His
weight disturbed the balance of the thing, it rolled over

ponderously, and as Kotuko sprang aside to avoid it, slid after him, squeaking and hissing on the ice-slope.

That was enough for Kotuko. He had been brought up to believe that every rock and boulder had its owner (its *inua*), who was generally a one-eyed kind of a Woman-Thing called a *tornaq*, and that when a *tornaq* meant to help a man she rolled after him inside her stone house, and asked him whether he would take her for a guardian spirit. (In summer thaws the ice-propped rocks and boulders roll and slip all over the face of the land, so you can easily see how the idea of live stones arose.) Kotuko heard the blood beating in his ears as he had heard it all day, and he thought that was the *tornaq* of the stone speaking to him. Before he reached home he was quite certain that he had held a long conversation with her, and as all his people believed that this was quite possible, no one contradicted him.

"She said to me, 'I jump down, I jump down from my place on the snow,' " cried Kotuko, with hollow eyes, leaning forward in the half-lighted hut. "She said, 'I will be a guide.' She says, 'I will guide you to the good seal-holes.' Tomorrow I go out, and the *tornaq* will guide me."

Then the *angekok*, the village sorcerer, came in, and Kotuko told him the tale a second time. It lost nothing in the telling.

"Follow the *tornait* [the spirits of the stones], and they will bring us food again," said the *angekok*.

Now the girl from the North had been lying near the lamp, eating very little and saying less for days past; but when Amoraq and Kadlu next morning packed and lashed a little hand-sleigh for Kotuko, and loaded it with his hunting-gear and as much blubber and frozen seal-meat as they could spare, she took the pulling-rope, and stepped out boldly at the boy's side.

"Your house is my house," she said, as the little bone-shod sleigh squeaked and bumped behind them in the awful Arctic night.

"My house is your house," said Kotuko; "but *I* think that we shall both go to Sedna together."

Now Sedna is the Mistress of the Underworld, and the Inuit believe that every one who dies must spend a year in her horrible country before going to Quadli-parmiut, the Happy Place, where it never freezes and the fat reindeer trot up when you call.

Through the village people were shouting: "The *tornait* have spoken to Kotuko. They will show him open ice. He will bring us the seal again!" Their voices were soon swallowed up by the cold, empty dark, and Kotuko and the girl shoulder close together as they strained on the pulling-rope or humoured the sleigh through the ice in the direction of the Polar Sea. Kotuko insisted that the *tornaq* of the stone had told him to go north, and north they went under Tuktuqd-jung the Reindeer—those stars that we call the Great Bear.

No European could have made five miles a day over the ice-rubbish and the sharp-edged drifts; but those two knew exactly the turn of the wrist that coaxes a sleigh round a hummock, the jerk that nearly lifts it out of an ice-crack, and the exact strength that goes to the few quiet strokes of the spear-head that make a path possible when everything looks hopeless.

The girl said nothing, but bowed her head, and the long wolverine-fur fringe of her ermine hood blew across her broad, dark face. The sky above them was an intense velvety black, changing to bands of Indian red on the horizon, where the great stars burned like street-lamps. From time to time a greenish wave of

the Northern Lights would roll across the hollow of
the high heavens, flick like a flag, and disappear; or a
meteor would crackle from darkness to darkness, trailing a shower of sparks behind. Then they could see
the ridged and furrowed surface of the floe tipped
and laced with strange colours—red, copper, and blu-
ish; but in the ordinary starlight everything turned to
one frost-bitten gray. The floe, as you will remember,
had been battered and tormented by the autumn gales
till it was one frozen earthquake. There were gullies
and ravines, and holes like gravel-pits, cut in ice; lumps
and scattered pieces frozen down to the original floor
of the floe; blotches of old black ice that had been
thrust under the floe in some gale and heaved up again;
roundish boulders of ice; saw-like edges of ice carved
by the snow that flies before the wind; and sunken pits
where thirty or forty acres lay below the level of the
rest of the field. From a little distance you might have
taken the lumps for seal or walrus, overturned sleighs
or men on a hunting expedition, or even the great Ten-
legged White Spirit-Bear himself; but in spite of these
fantastic shapes, all on the very edge of starting into
life, there was neither sound nor the least faint echo of
sound. And through this silence and through this
waste, where the sudden lights flapped and went out
again, the sleigh and the two that pulled it crawled like
things in a nightmare—a nightmare of the end of the
world at the end of the world.

When they were tired Kotuko would make what
the hunters call a "half-house," a very small snow hut,
into which they would huddle with the travelling-
lamp, and try to thaw out the frozen seal-meat. When
they had slept, the march began again—thirty miles a
day to get ten miles northward. The girl was always
very silent, but Kotuko muttered to himself and broke

out into songs he had learned in the Singing-House—
summer songs, and reindeer and salmon songs—all horribly out of place at that season. He would declare
that he heard the *tornaq* growling to him, and would
run wildly up a hummock, tossing his arms and speaking in loud, threatening tones. To tell the truth,
Kotuko was very nearly crazy for the time being; but
the girl was sure that he was being guided by his
guardian spirit, and that everything would come right.
She was not surprised, therefore, when at the end of
the fourth march Kotuko, whose eyes were burning
like fire-balls in his head, told her that his *tornaq* was
following them across the snow in the shape of a two-
headed dog. The girl looked where Kotuko pointed,
and something seemed to slip into a ravine. It was certainly not human, but everybody knew that the *tornait* preferred to appear in the shape of bear and seal,
and such like.

It might have been the Ten-legged White Spirit-
Bear himself, or it might have been anything, for
Kotuko and the girl were so starved that their eyes
were untrustworthy. They had trapped nothing, and
seen no trace of game since they had left the village;
their food would not hold out for another week, and
there was a gale coming. A Polar storm can blow for
ten days without a break, and all that while it is certain
death to be abroad. Kotuko laid up a snow-house large
enough to take in the hand-sleigh (never be separated
from your meat), and while he was shaping the last
irregular block of ice that makes the key-stone of the
roof, he saw a Thing looking at him from a little cliff
of ice half a mile away. The air was hazy, and the
Thing seemed to be forty feet long and ten feet high,
with twenty feet of tail and a shape that quivered all

along the outlines. The girl saw it too, but instead of
crying aloud with terror, said quietly, "That is Quiquern. What comes after?"

"He will speak to me," said Kotuko; but the snow-
knife trembled in his hand as he spoke, because however much a man may believe that he is a friend of
strange and ugly spirits, he seldom likes to be taken
quite at his word. Quiquern, too, is the phantom of
a gigantic toothless dog without any hair, who is supposed to live in the far North, and to wander about the
country just before things are going to happen. They
may be pleasant or unpleasant things, but not even the
sorcerers care to speak about Quiquern. He makes the
dogs go mad. Like the Spirit-Bear, he has several extra
pairs of legs,—six or eight,—and this Thing jumping up
and down in the haze had more legs than any real dog
needed. Kotuko and the girl huddled into their hut
quickly. Of course if Quiquern had wanted them, he
could have torn it to pieces above their heads, but the
sense of a foot-thick snow-wall between themselves
and the wicked dark was great comfort. The gale
broke with the shriek of wind like the shriek of a train,
and for three days and three nights it held, never vary-
ing one point, and never lulling even for a minute.
They fed the stone lamp between their knees, and
nibbled at the half-warm seal-meat, and watched the
black soot gather on the roof for seventy-two long
hours. The girl counted up the food in the sleigh;
there was not more than two days' supply, and Kotuko looked over the iron heads and the deer-sinew
fastenings of his harpoon and his seal-lance and his
bird-dart. There was nothing else to do.

"We shall go to Sedna soon—very soon," the girl
whispered. "In three days we shall lie down and go.

Will your *tornaq* do nothing? Sing her an *angekok's* song to make her come here."

He began to sing in the high-pitched howl of the magic songs, and the gale went down slowly. In the middle of his song the girl started, laid her mittened hand and then her head to the ice floor of the hut. Kotuko followed her example, and the two kneeled, staring into each other's eyes, and listening with every nerve. He ripped a thin sliver of whalebone from the rim of a bird-snare that lay on the sleigh, and, after straightening, set it upright in a little hole in the ice, firming it down with his mitten. It was almost as delicately adjusted as a compass-needle, and now instead of listening they watched. The thin rod quivered a little—the least little jar in the world; then it vibrated steadily for a few seconds, came to rest, and vibrated again, this time nodding to another point of the compass.

"Too soon!" said Kotuko. "Some big floe has broken far away outside."

The girl pointed at the rod, and shook her head. "It is the big breaking," she said. "Listen to the ground-ice. It knocks."

When they kneeled this time they heard the most curious muffled grunts and knockings, apparently under their feet. Sometimes it sounded as though a blind puppy were squeaking above the lamp; then as if a stone were being ground on hard ice; and again, like muffled blows on a drum; but all dragged out and made small, as though they travelled through a little horn a weary distance away.

"We shall not go to Sedna lying down," said Kotuko. "It is the breaking. The *tornaq* has cheated us. We shall die."

All this may sound absurd enough, but the two were

face to face with a very real danger. The three days' gale had driven the deep water of Baffin's Bay southerly, and piled it on to the edge of the far-reaching land-ice that stretches from Bylot's Island to the west. Also, the strong current which sets east out of Lancaster Sound carried with it mile upon mile of what they call pack-ice—rough ice that has not frozen into fields; and this pack was bombarding the floe at the same time that the swell and heave of the storm-worked sea was weakening and undermining it. What Kotuko and the girl had been listening to were the faint echoes of that fight thirty or forty miles away, and the little tell-tale rod quivered to the shock of it.

Now, as the Inuit say, when the ice once wakes after its long winter sleep, there is no knowing what may happen, for solid floe-ice changes shape almost as quickly as a cloud. The gale was evidently a spring gale sent out of time, and anything was possible.

Yet the two were happier in their minds than before. If the floe broke up there would be no more waiting and suffering. Spirits, goblins, and witch-people were moving about on the racking ice, and they might find themselves stepping into Sedna's country side by side with all sorts of wild Things, the flush of excitement still on them. When they left the hut after the gale, the noise on the horizon was steadily growing, and the tough ice moaned and buzzed all round them.

"It is still waiting," said Kotuko.

On the top of a hummock sat or crouched the eight-legged Thing that they had seen three days before—and it howled horribly.

"Let us follow," said the girl. "It may know some way that does not lead to Sedna"; but she reeled from weakness as she took the pulling-rope. The Thing

moved off slowly and clumsily across the ridges, heading always toward the westward and the land, and
they followed, while the growling thunder at the edge
of the floe rolled nearer and nearer. The floe's lip was
split and cracked in every direction for three or four
miles inland, and great pans of ten-foot-thick ice, from
a few yards to twenty acres square, were jolting and
ducking and surging into one another, and into the
yet unbroken floe, as the heavy swell took and shook
and spouted between them. This battering-ram ice
was, so to speak, the first army that the sea was flinging against the floe. The incessant crash and jar of
these cakes almost drowned the ripping sound of
sheets of pack-ice driven bodily under the floe as cards
are hastily pushed under a tablecloth. Where the
water was shallow these sheets would be piled one
atop of the other till the bottommost touched mud
fifty feet down, and the discoloured sea banked behind
the muddy ice till the increasing pressure drove all
forward again. In addition to the floe and the pack-
ice, the gale and the currents were bringing down true
bergs, sailing mountains of ice, snapped off from the
Greenland side of the water or the north shore of Melville Bay. They pounded in solemnly, the waves breaking white round them, and advanced on the floe like
an old-time fleet under full sail. A berg that seemed
ready to carry the world before it would ground
helplessly in deep water, reel over, and wallow in a
lather of foam and mud and flying frozen spray, while
a much smaller and lower one would rip and ride into
the flat floe, flinging tons of ice on either side, and
cutting a track half a mile long before it was stopped.
Some fell like swords, sheering a raw-edged canal; and
others splintered into a shower of blocks, weighing
scores of tons apiece, that whirled and skirled among

the hummocks. Others, again, rose up bodily out of
the water when they shoaled, twisted as though in
pain, and fell solidly on their sides, while the sea
threshed over their shoulders. This trampling and
crowding and bending and buckling and arching of
the ice into every possible shape was going on as far
as the eye could reach all along the north line of the
floe. From where Kotuko and the girl were, the confusion looked no more than an uneasy, rippling, crawling movement under the horizon; but it came toward
them each moment, and they could hear, far away to
landward, a heavy booming, as it might have been the
boom of artillery through a fog. That showed that the
floe was being jammed home against the iron cliffs of
Bylot's Island, the land to the southward behind them.

"This has never been before," said Kotuko, staring
stupidly. "This is not the time. How can the floe break
now?"

"Follow *that!*" the girl cried, pointing to the Thing
half limping, half running distractedly before them.
They followed, tugging at the hand-sleigh, while
nearer and nearer came the roaring march of the ice.
At last the fields round them cracked and starred in
every direction, and the cracks opened and snapped
like the teeth of wolves. But where the Thing rested,
on a mound of old and scattered ice-blocks some fifty
feet high, there was no motion. Kotuko leaped forward wildly, dragging the girl after him, and crawled
to the bottom of the mound. The talking of the ice
grew louder and louder round them, but the mound
stayed fast, and, as the girl looked at him, he threw his
right elbow upward and outward, making the Inuit
sign for land in the shape of an island. And land it was
that the eight-legged, limping Thing had led them to
—some granite-tipped, sand-beached islet off the coast,

shod and sheathed and masked with ice so that no man could have told it from the floe, but at the bottom solid earth, and not shifting ice! The smashing and rebound of the floes as they grounded and splintered marked the borders of it, and a friendly shoal ran out to the northward, and turned aside the rush of the heaviest ice, exactly as a ploughshare turns over loam. There was danger, of course, that some heavily squeezed ice-field might shoot up the beach, and plane off the top of the islet bodily; but that did not trouble Kotuko and the girl when they made their snow-house and began to eat, and heard the ice hammer and skid along the beach. The Thing had disappeared, and Kotuko was talking excitedly about his power over spirits as he crouched round the lamp. In the middle of his wild sayings the girl began to laugh, and rock herself backward and forward.

Behind her shoulder, crawling into the hut crawl by crawl, there were two heads, one yellow and one black, that belonged to two of the most sorrowful and ashamed dogs that ever you saw. Kotuko the dog was one, and the black leader was the other. Both were now fat, well-looking, and quite restored to their proper minds, but coupled to each other in an extraordinary fashion. When the black leader ran off, you remember, his harness was still on him. He must have met Kotuko the dog, and played or fought with him, for his shoulder-loop had caught in the plaited copper wire of Kotuko's collar, and had drawn tight, so that neither could get at the trace to gnaw it apart, but each was fastened sidelong to his neighbour's neck. That, with the freedom of hunting on their own account, must have helped to cure their madness. They were very sober.

The girl pushed the two shamefaced creatures towards Kotuko, and, sobbing with laughter, cried, "That is Quiquern, who led us to safe ground. Look at his eight legs and double head!"

Kotuko cut them free, and they fell into his arms, yellow and black together, trying to explain how they had got their senses back again. Kotuko ran a hand down their ribs, which were round and well clothed. "They have found food," he said, with a grin. "I do not think we shall go to Sedna so soon. My *tornaq* sent these. The sickness has left them."

As soon as they had greeted Kotuko, these two, who had been forced to sleep and eat and hunt together for the past few weeks, flew at each other's throat, and there was a beautiful battle in the snow-house. "Empty dogs do not fight," Kotuko said. "They have found the seal. Let us sleep. We shall find food."

When they waked there was open water on the north beach of the island, and all the loosened ice had been driven landward. The first sound of the surf is one of the most delightful that the Inuit can hear, for it means that spring is on the road. Kotuko and the girl took hold of hands and smiled, for the clear, full roar of the surge among the ice reminded them of salmon and reindeer time and the smell of blossoming ground-willows. Even as they looked, the sea began to skim over between the floating cakes of ice, so intense was the cold; but on the horizon there was a vast red glare, and that was the light of the sunken sun. It was more like hearing him yawn in his sleep than seeing him rise, and the glare lasted for only a few minutes, but it marked the turn of the year. Nothing, they felt, could alter that.

Kotuko found the dogs fighting over a fresh-killed seal who was following the fish that a gale always

disturbs. He was the first of some twenty or thirty
seal that landed on the island in the course of the day,
and till the sea froze hard there were hundreds of keen
black heads rejoicing in the shallow free water and
floating about with the floating ice.

It was good to eat seal-liver again; to fill the lamps
recklessly with blubber, and watch the flame blaze
three feet in the air; but as soon as the new sea-ice
bore, Kotuko and the girl loaded the hand-sleigh, and
made the two dogs pull as they had never pulled in
their lives, for they feared what might have happened
in their village. The weather was as pitiless as usual;
but it is easier to draw a sleigh loaded with good food
than to hunt starving. They left five-and-twenty seal
carcasses buried in the ice of the beach, all ready for
use, and hurried back to their people. The dogs
showed them the way as soon as Kotuko told them
what was expected, and though there was no sign of
a landmark, in two days they were giving tongue outside Kadlu's house. Only three dogs answered them;
the others had been eaten, and the houses were all dark.
But when Kotuko shouted, "Ojo!" (boiled meat),
weak voices replied, and when he called the muster
of the village name by name, very distinctly, there
were no gaps in it.

An hour later the lamps blazed in Kadlu's house;
snow-water was heating; the pots were beginning to
simmer, and the snow was dripping from the roof, as
Amoraq made ready a meal for all the village, and
the boy-baby in the hood chewed at a strip of rich
nutty blubber, and the hunters slowly and methodi-
cally filled themselves to the very brim with seal-meat.
Kotuko and the girl told their tale. The two dogs sat
between them, and whenever their names came in,
they cocked an ear apiece and looked most thoroughly

"HE SKY ABOVE THEM WAS AN INTENSE VELVETY BLACK . . ." (*page 128*)

ashamed of themselves. A dog who has once gone mad
and recovered, the Inuit say, is safe against all further
attacks.

"So the *tornaq* did not forget us," said Kotuko.
"The storm blew, the ice broke, and the seal swam
in behind the fish that were frightened by the storm.
Now the new seal-holes are not two days distant. Let
the good hunters go to-morrow and bring back the
seal I have speared—twenty-five seal buried in the ice.
When we have eaten those we will all follow the seal
on the floe."

"What do *you* do?" said the sorcerer in the same
sort of voice as he used to Kadlu, richest of the
Tununirmiut.

Kadlu looked at the girl from the North, and said
quietly, "*We* build a house." He pointed to the north-
west side of Kadlu's house, for that is the side on
which the married son or daughter always lives.

The girl turned her hands palm upward, with a little
despairing shake of her head. She was a foreigner,
picked up starving, and could bring nothing to the
housekeeping.

Amoraq jumped from the bench where she sat, and
began to sweep things into the girl's lap—stone lamps,
iron skin-scrapers, tin kettles, deer-skins embroidered
with musk-ox teeth, and real canvas-needles such as
sailors use—the finest dowry that has ever been given
on the far edge of the Arctic Circle, and the girl from
the North bowed her head down to the very floor.

"Also these!" said Kotuko, laughing and signing to
the dogs, who thrust their cold muzzles into the girl's
face.

"Ah," said the *angekok*, with an important cough,
as though he had been thinking it all over. "As soon
as Kotuko left the village I went to the Singing-House

and sang magic. I sang all the long nights, and called upon the Spirit of the Reindeer. *My* singing made the gale blow that broke the ice and drew the two dogs toward Kotuko when the ice would have crushed his bones. *My* song drew the seal in behind the broken ice. My body lay still in the *quaggi*, but my spirit ran about on the ice, and guided Kotuko and the dogs in all the things they did. I did it."

Everybody was full and sleepy, so no one contradicted; and the *angekok*, by virtue of his office, helped himself to yet another lump of boiled meat, and lay down to sleep with the others in the warm, well-lighted, oil-smelling home.

.   .   .   .   .

Now Kotuko, who drew very well in the Inuit fashion, scratched pictures of all these adventures on a long, flat piece of ivory with a hole at one end. When he and the girl went north to Ellesmere Land in the year of the Wonderful Open Winter, he left the picture-story with Kadlu, who lost it in the shingle when his dog-sleigh broke down one summer on the beach of Lake Netilling at Nikosiring, and there a Lake Inuit found it next spring and sold it to a man at Imigen who was interpreter on a Cumberland Sound whaler, and he sold it to Hans Olsen, who was afterward a quartermaster on board a big steamer that took tourists to the North Cape in Norway. When the tourist season was over, the steamer ran between London and Australia, stopping at Ceylon, and there Olsen sold the ivory to a Cingalese jeweller for two imitation sapphires. I found it under some rubbish in a house at Colombo, and have translated it from one end to the other.

"ANGUTIVAUN TAINA"

[This is a very free translation of the Song of the Returning Hunter, as the men used to sing it after seal-spearing. The Inuit always repeat things over and over again.]

Our gloves are stiff with the frozen blood,
    Our furs with the drifted snow,
As we come in with the seal—the seal!
    In from the edge of the floe.

Au jana! Aua! Oha! Haq!
    And the yelping dog-teams go,
And the long whips crack, and the men come back,
    Back from the edge of the floe!

We tracked our seal to his secret place,
    We heard him scratch below,
We made our mark, and we watched beside,
    Out on the edge of the floe.

We raised our lance when he rose to breathe,
    We drove it downward—so!
And we played him thus, and we killed him thus,
    Out on the edge of the floe.

Our gloves are glued with the frozen blood,
Our eyes with the drifting snow;
But we come back to our wives again,
Back from the edge of the floe!

Au jana! Aua! Oha! Haq!
And the loaded dog-teams go,
And the wives can hear their men come back,
Back from the edge of the floe!

TOOMAI OF THE ELEPHANTS

TOOMAI OF THE ELEPHANTS

*I will remember what I was. I am sick of rope and
   chain.
  I will remember my old strength and all my forest
    affairs.
I will not sell my back to man for a bundle of sugar-
   cane,
  I will go out to my own kind, and the wood-folk
    in their lairs.*

*I will go out until the day, until the morning break,
  Out to the winds' untainted kiss, the waters' clean
    caress:
I will forget my ankle-ring and snap my picket-stake.
  I will revisit my lost loves, and playmates masterless!*

KALA NAG, which means Black Snake, had served
the Indian Government in every way that an elephant
could serve it for forty-seven years, and as he was
fully twenty years old when he was caught, that
makes him nearly seventy—a ripe age for an elephant.
He remembered pushing, with a big leather pad on
his forehead, at a gun stuck in deep mud, and that was
before the Afghan War of 1842, and he had not then
come to his full strength. His mother, Radha Pyari,—

Radha the darling,—who had been caught in the same drive with Kala Nag, told him, before his little milk tusks had dropped out, that elephants who were afraid always got hurt; and Kala Nag knew that that advice was good, for the first time that he saw a shell burst he backed, screaming, into a stand of piled rifles, and the bayonets pricked him in all his softest places. So before he was twenty-five he gave up being afraid, and so he was the best-loved and the best-looked-after elephant in the service of the Government of India. He had carried tents, twelve hundred pounds' weight of tents, on the march in Upper India; he had been hoisted into a ship at the end of a steam-crane and taken for days across the water, and made to carry a mortar on his back in a strange and rocky country very far from India, and had seen the Emperor Theodore lying dead in Magdala, and had come back again in the steamer, entitled, so the soldiers said, to the Abyssinian War medal. He had seen his fellow-elephants die of cold and epilepsy and starvation and sunstroke up at a place called Ali Musjid, ten years later; and afterward he had been sent down thousands of miles south to haul and pile big baulks of teak in the timber-yards at Moulmein. There he had half killed an insubordinate young elephant who was shirking his fair share of the work.

After that he was taken off timber-hauling, and employed, with a few score other elephants who were trained to the business, in helping to catch wild elephants among the Garo hills. Elephants are very strictly preserved by the Indian Government. There is one whole department which does nothing else but hunt them, and catch them, and break them in, and send them up and down the country as they are needed for work.

Kala Nag stood ten fair feet at the shoulders, and his tusks had been cut off short at five feet, and bound round the ends, to prevent them splitting with bands of copper; but he could do more with those stumps than any untrained elephant could do with the real sharpened ones.

When, after weeks and weeks of cautious driving of scattered elephants across the hills, the forty or fifty wild monsters were driven into the last stockade, and the big drop-gate, made of tree-trunks lashed together, jarred down behind them, Kala Nag, at the word of command, would go into that flaring, trumpeting pandemonium (generally at night, when the flicker of the torches made it difficult to judge distances), and, picking out the biggest and wildest tusker of the mob would hammer him and hustle him into quiet while the men on the backs of the other elephants roped and tied the smaller ones.

There was nothing in the way of fighting that Kala Nag, the old wise Black Snake, did not know, for he had stood up more than once in his time to the charge of the wounded tiger, and, curling up his soft trunk to be out of harm's way, had knocked the springing brute sideways in mid-air with a quick sickle-cut of his head, that he had invented all by himself; had knocked him over, and kneeled upon him with his huge knees till the life went out with a gasp and a howl, and there was only a fluffy striped thing on the ground for Kala Nag to pull by the tail.

"Yes," said Big Toomai, his driver, the son of Black Toomai who had taken him to Abyssinia, and grandson of Toomai of the Elephants who had seen him caught, "there is nothing that the Black Snake fears except me. He has seen three generations of us feed him and groom him, and he will live to see four."

"He is afraid of *me* also," said Little Toomai, standing up to his full height of four feet, with only one rag upon him. He was ten years old, the eldest son of Big Toomai, and, according to custom, he would take his father's place on Kala Nag's neck when he grew up, and would handle the heavy iron *ankus*, the elephant-goad that had been worn smooth by his father, and his grandfather, and his great-grandfather. He knew what he was talking of; for he had been born under Kala Nag's shadow, had played with the end of his trunk before he could walk, had taken him down to water as soon as he could walk, and Kala Nag would no more have dreamed of disobeying his shrill little orders than he would have dreamed of killing him on that day when Big Toomai carried the little brown baby under Kala Nag's tusks, and told him to salute his master that was to be.

"Yes," said Little Toomai, "he is afraid of *me*," and he took long strides up to Kala Nag, called him a fat old pig, and made him lift up his feet one after the other.

"Wah!" said Little Toomai, "thou art a big elephant," and he wagged his fluffy head, quoting his father. "The Government may pay for elephants, but they belong to us mahouts. When thou art old, Kala Nag, there will come some rich Rajah, and he will buy thee from the Government, on account of thy size and thy manners, and then thou wilt have nothing to do but to carry gold earrings in thy ears, and a gold howdah on thy back, and a red cloth covered with gold on thy sides, and walk at the head of the processions of the King. Then I shall sit on thy neck, O Kala Nag, with a silver *ankus*, and men will run before us with golden sticks, crying 'Room for the King's ele-

phant!' That will be good, Kala Nag, but not so good as this hunting in the jungles."

"Umph!" said Big Toomai. "Thou art a boy, and as wild as a buffalo-calf. This running up and down among the hills is not the best Government service. I am getting old, and I do not love wild elephants. Give me brick elephant-lines, one stall to each elephant, and big stumps to tie them to safely, and flat, broad roads to exercise upon, instead of this come-and-go camping. Aha, the Cawnpore barracks were good. There was a bazaar close by, and only three hours' work a day."

Little Toomai remembered the Cawnpore elephant-lines and said nothing. He very much preferred the camp life, and hated those broad, flat roads, with the daily grubbing for grass in the forage-reserve, and the long hours when there was nothing to do except to watch Kala Nag fidgeting in his pickets.

What Little Toomai liked was the scramble up bridle-paths that only an elephant could take; the dip into the valley below; the glimpses of the wild elephants browsing miles away; the rush of the frightened pig and peacock under Kala Nag's feet; the blinding warm rains, when all the hills and valleys smoked; the beautiful misty mornings when nobody knew where they would camp that night; the steady, cautious drive of the wild elephants, and the mad rush and blaze and hullabaloo of the last night's drive, when the elephants poured into the stockade like boulders in a landslide, found that they could not get out, and flung themselves at the heavy posts only to be driven back by yells and flaring torches and volleys of blank cartridge.

Even a little boy could be of use there, and Toomai was as useful as three boys. He would get his torch

and wave it, and yell with the best. But the really good
time came when the driving out began, and the Keddah—that is, the stockade—looked like a picture of the
end of the world, and men had to make signs to one
another, because they could not hear themselves speak.
Then Little Toomai would climb up to the top of one
of the quivering stockade-posts, his sun-bleached
brown hair flying loose all over his shoulders, and he
looking like a goblin in the torch-light; and as soon as
there was a lull you could hear his high-pitched yells
of encouragement to Kala Nag, above the trumpeting
and crashing, and snapping of ropes, and groans of the
tethered elephants. "*Maîl, maîl, Kala Nag!* (Go on, go
on, Black Snake!) *Dant do!* (Give him the tusk!)
Somalo! Somalo! (Careful, careful!) *Maro! Mar!* (Hit
him, hit him!) Mind the post! *Arre! Arre! Hai!
Yai! Kya-a-ah!*" he would shout, and the big fight
between Kala Nag and the wild elephant would sway
to and fro across the Keddah, and the old elephant-
catchers would wipe the sweat out of their eyes, and
find time to nod to Little Toomai wriggling with joy
on the top of the posts.

He did more than wriggle. One night he slid down
from the post and slipped in between the elephants,
and threw up the loose end of a rope, which had
dropped, to a driver who was trying to get a purchase
on the leg of a kicking young calf (calves always give
more trouble than full-grown animals). Kala Nag saw
him, caught him in his trunk, and handed him up to
Big Toomai, who slapped him then and there, and put
him back on the post.

Next morning he gave him a scolding, and said:
"Are not good brick elephant-lines and a little tent-
carrying enough, that thou must needs go elephant-
catching on thy own account, little worthless? Now

those foolish hunters, whose pay is less than my pay, have spoken to Petersen Sahib of the matter." Little Toomai was frightened. He did not know much of white men, but Petersen Sahib was the greatest white man in the world to him. He was the head of all the Keddah operations—the man who caught all the elephants for the Government of India, and who knew more about the ways of elephants than any living man.

"What—what will happen?" said Little Toomai.

"Happen! the worst that can happen. Petersen Sahib is a madman. Else why should he go hunting these wild devils? He may even require thee to be an elephant-catcher, to sleep anywhere in these fever-filled jungles, and at last to be trampled to death in the Keddah. It is well that this nonsense ends safely. Next week the catching is over, and we of the plains are sent back to our stations. Then we will march on smooth roads, and forget all this hunting. But, son, I am angry that thou shouldst meddle in the business that belongs to these dirty Assamese jungle-folk. Kala Nag will obey none but me, so I must go with him into the Keddah; but he is only a fighting elephant, and he does not help to rope them. So I sit at my ease, as befits a mahout,—not a mere hunter,—a mahout, I say, and a man who gets a pension at the end of his service. Is the family of Toomai of the Elephants to be trodden underfoot in the dirt of a Keddah? Bad one! Wicked one! Worthless son! Go and wash Kala Nag and attend to his ears, and see that there are no thorns in his feet; or else Petersen Sahib will surely catch thee and make thee a wild hunter—a follower of elephants' foot-tracks, a jungle-bear. Bah! Shame! Go!"

Little Toomai went off without saying a word, but he told Kala Nag all his grievances while he was examining his feet. "No matter," said Little Toomai, turning up the fringe of Kala Nag's huge right ear. "They have said my name to Petersen Sahib, and perhaps—and perhaps—and perhaps—who knows? Hai! That is a big thorn that I have pulled out!"

The next few days were spent in getting the elephants together, in walking the newly caught wild elephants up and down between a couple of tame ones, to prevent them from giving too much trouble on the downward march to the plains, and in taking stock of the blankets and ropes and things that had been worn out or lost in the forest.

Petersen Sahib came in on his clever she-elephant Pudmini. He had been paying off other camps among the hills, for the season was coming to an end, and there was a native clerk sitting at a table under a tree to pay the drivers their wages. As each man was paid he went back to his elephant, and joined the line that stood ready to start. The catchers, and hunters, and beaters, the men of the regular Keddah, who stayed in the jungle year in and year out, sat on the backs of the elephants that belonged to Petersen Sahib's permanent force, or leaned against the trees with their guns across their arms, and made fun of the drivers who were going away, and laughed when the newly caught elephants broke the line and ran about.

Big Toomai went up to the clerk with Little Toomai behind him, and Machua Appa, the head-tracker, said in an undertone to a friend of his, "There goes one piece of good elephant-stuff at least. 'Tis a pity to send that young jungle-cock to moult in the plains."

Now Petersen Sahib had ears all over him, as a man must have who listens to the most silent of all living things—the wild elephant. He turned where he was lying all along on Pudmini's back, and said, "What is that? I did not know of a man among the plains-

drivers who had wit enough to rope even a dead elephant."

"This is not a man, but a boy. He went into the
Keddah at the last drive, and threw Barmao there the
rope when we were trying to get that young calf with
the blotch on his shoulder away from his mother."

Machua Appa pointed at Little Toomai, and Petersen Sahib looked, and Little Toomai bowed to the
earth.

"He throw a rope? He is smaller than a picket-pin.
Little one, what is thy name?" said Petersen Sahib.

Little Toomai was too frightened to speak, but Kala
Nag was behind him, and Toomai made a sign with
his hand, and the elephant caught him up in his trunk
and held him level with Pudmini's forehead, in front
of the great Petersen Sahib. Then Little Toomai
covered his face with his hands, for he was only a
child, and except where elephants were concerned,
he was just as bashful as a child could be.

"Oho!" said Petersen Sahib, smiling underneath his
moustache, "and why didst thou teach thy elephant
that trick? Was it to help thee steal green corn from
the roofs of the houses when the ears are put out to
dry?"

"Not green corn, Protector of the Poor,—melons,"
said Little Toomai, and all the men sitting about broke
into a roar of laughter. Most of them had taught their
elephants that trick when they were boys. Little Toomai was hanging eight feet up in the air, and he wished
very much that he were eight feet underground.

"He is Toomai, my son, Sahib," said Big Toomai,
scowling. "He is a very bad boy, and he will end in a
jail, Sahib."

"Of that I have my doubts," said Petersen Sahib. "A
boy who can face a full Keddah at his age does not

end in jails. See, little one, here are four annas to spend in sweetmeats because thou hast a little head under that great thatch of hair. In time thou mayest become a hunter too." Big Toomai scowled more than ever. "Remember, though, that Keddahs are not good for children to play in," Petersen Sahib went on.

"Must I never go there, Sahib?" asked Little Toomai, with a big gasp.

"Yes." Petersen Sahib smiled again. "When thou hast seen the elephants dance. That is the proper time. Come to me when thou hast seen the elephants dance, and then I will let thee go into all the Keddahs."

There was another roar of laughter, for that is an old joke among elephant-catchers, and it means just never. There are great cleared flat places hidden away in the forests that are called elephants' ball-rooms, but even these are only found by accident, and no man has ever seen the elephants dance. When a driver boasts of his skill and bravery the other drivers say, "And when didst *thou* see the elephants dance?"

Kala Nag put Little Toomai down, and he bowed to the earth again and went away with his father, and gave the silver four-anna piece to his mother, who was nursing his baby-brother, and they all were put up on Kala Nag's back, and the line of grunting, squealing elephants rolled down the hill-path to the plains. It was a very lively march on account of the new elephants, who gave trouble at every ford, and who needed coaxing or beating every other minute.

Big Toomai prodded Kala Nag spitefully, for he was very angry, but Little Toomai was too happy to speak. Petersen Sahib had noticed him, and given him money, so he felt as a private soldier would feel if he had been called out of the ranks and praised by his commander-in-chief.

"What did Petersen Sahib mean by the elephant-dance?" he said, at last, softly to his mother.

Big Toomai heard him and grunted. "That thou shouldst never be one of these hill-buffaloes of trackers. *That* was what he meant. Oh you in front, what is blocking the way?"

An Assamese driver, two or three elephants ahead, turned round angrily, crying: "Bring up Kala Nag, and knock this youngster of mine into good behaviour. Why should Petersen Sahib have chosen *me* to go down with you donkeys of the rice-fields? Lay your beast alongside, Toomai, and let him prod with his tusks. By all the Gods of the Hills, these new elephants are possessed, or else they can smell their companions in the jungle."

Kala Nag hit the new elephant in the ribs and knocked the wind out of him, as Big Toomai said, "We have swept the hills of wild elephants at the last catch. It is only your carelessness in driving. Must I keep order along the whole line?"

"Hear him!" said the other driver. "*We* have swept the hills! Ho! ho! You are very wise, you plains-people. Any one but a mud-head who never saw the jungle would know that *they* know that the drives are ended for the season. Therefore all the wild elephants to-night will——but why should I waste wisdom on a river-turtle?"

"What will they do?" Little Toomai called out.

"*Ohé*, little one. Art thou there? Well, I will tell thee, for thou hast a cool head. They will dance, and it behooves thy father, who has swept *all* the hills of *all* the elephants, to double-chain his pickets to-night."

"What talk is this?" said Big Toomai. "For forty years, father and son, we have tended elephants, and we have never heard such moonshine about dances."

"Yes; but a plains-man who lives in a hut knows only the four walls of his hut. Well, leave thy elephants unshackled to-night and see what comes; as for their dancing, I have seen the place where——*Bapree-Bap!* how many windings has the Dihang River? Here is another ford, and we must swim the calves. Stop still, you behind there."

And in this way, talking and wrangling and splashing through the rivers, they made their first march to a sort of receiving-camp for the new elephants; but they lost their tempers long before they got there.

Then the elephants were chained by their hind legs to their big stumps of pickets, and extra ropes were fitted to the new elephants, and the fodder was piled before them, and the hill-drivers went back to Petersen Sahib through the afternoon light, telling the plains-drivers to be extra careful that night, and laughing when the plains-drivers asked the reason.

Little Toomai attended to Kala Nag's supper, and as evening fell wandered through the camp, unspeakably happy, in search of a tom-tom. When an Indian child's heart is full, he does not run about and make a noise in an irregular fashion. He sits down to a sort of revel all by himself. And Little Toomai had been spoken to by Petersen Sahib! If he had not found what he wanted I believe he would have burst. But the sweetmeat-seller in the camp lent him a little tom-tom —a drum beaten with the flat of the hand—and he sat down, cross-legged, before Kala Nag as the stars began to come out, the tom-tom in his lap, and he thumped and he thumped and he thumped, and the more he thought of the great honour that had been done to him, the more he thumped, all alone among the elephant-fodder. There was no tune and no words, but the thumping made him happy.

The new elephants strained at their ropes, and squealed and trumpeted from time to time, and he could hear his mother in the camp hut putting his small brother to sleep with an old, old song about the great God Shiv, who once told all the animals what they should eat. It is a very soothing lullaby, and the first verse says:

Shiv, who poured the harvest and made the winds
        to blow,
Sitting at the doorways of a day of long ago,
Gave to each his portion, food and toil and fate,
From the King upon the guddee *to the Beggar at*
        the gate.
    All things made he—Shiva the Preserver.
    Mahadeo! Mahadeo! He made all,—
    Thorn for the camel, fodder for the kine,
    And mother's heart for sleepy head, O little son
        of mine!

Little Toomai came in with a joyous *tunk-a-tunk* at the end of each verse, till he felt sleepy and stretched himself on the fodder at Kala Nag's side.

At last the elephants began to lie down one after another, as is their custom, till only Kala Nag at the right of the line was left standing up; and he rocked slowly from side to side, his ears put forward to listen to the night wind as it blew very slowly across the hills. The air was full of all the night noises that, taken together, make one big silence—the click of one bamboo-stem against the other, the rustle of something alive in the undergrowth, the scratch and squawk of a half-waked bird (birds are awake in the night much more often than we imagine), and the fall of water ever so far away. Little Toomai slept for some time, and when he waked it was brilliant moonlight, and Kala Nag was still standing up with his ears cocked. Little Toomai turned, rustling in the fodder, and watched the curve of his big back against half the stars in heaven; and while he watched he heard, so far away that it sounded no more than a pinhole of noise pricked through the stillness, the "hoot-toot" of a wild elephant.

All the elephants in the lines jumped up as if they had been shot, and their grunts at last waked the sleeping mahouts, and they came out and drove in the picket-pegs with big mallets, and tightened this rope and knotted that till all was quiet. One new elephant had nearly grubbed up his picket, and Big Toomai took off Kala Nag's leg-chain and shackled that elephant fore-foot to hind-foot, but slipped a loop of grass-string round Kala Nag's leg, and told him to remember that he was tied fast. He knew that he and his father and his grandfather had done the very same thing hundreds of times before. Kala Nag did not answer to the order by gurgling, as he usually did. He stood still, looking out across the moonlight, his head a little raised, and his ears spread like fans, up to the great folds of the Garo hills.

"Look to him if he grows restless in the night," said Big Toomai to Little Toomai, and he went into the hut and slept. Little Toomai was just going to sleep, too, when he heard the coir string snap with a little "tang," and Kala Nag rolled out of his pickets as slowly and as silently as a cloud rolls out of the mouth of a valley. Little Toomai pattered after him, barefooted, down the road in the moonlight, calling under his breath, "Kala Nag! Kala Nag! Take me with you, O Kala Nag!" The elephant turned without a sound, took three strides back to the boy in the moonlight,

put down his trunk, swung him up to his neck, and almost before Little Toomai had settled his knees slipped into the forest.

There was one blast of furious trumpeting from the lines, and then silence shut down on everything, and Kala Nag began to move. Sometimes a tuft of high grass washed along his sides as a wave washes along the sides of a ship, and sometimes a cluster of wild-pepper vines would scrape along his back, or a bamboo would creak where his shoulder touched it; but between those times he moved absolutely without any sound, drifting through the thick Garo forest as though it had been smoke. He was going uphill, but though Little Toomai watched the stars in the rifts of the trees, he could not tell in what direction.

Then Kala Nag reached the crest of the ascent and stopped for a minute, and Little Toomai could see the tops of the trees lying all speckled and furry under the moonlight for miles and miles, and the blue-white mist over the river in the hollow. Toomai leaned forward and looked, and he felt that the forest was awake below him—awake and alive and crowded. A big brown fruit-eating bat brushed past his ear; a porcupine's quills rattled in the thicket; and in the darkness between the tree-stems he heard a hog-bear digging hard in the moist, warm earth, and snuffing as it digged.

Then the branches closed over his head again, and Kala Nag began to go down into the valley—not quietly this time, but as a runaway gun goes down a steep bank—in one rush. The huge limbs moved as steadily as pistons, eight feet to each stride, and the wrinkled skin of the elbow-points rustled. The undergrowth on either side of him ripped with a noise like torn canvas, and the saplings that he heaved away right and left with his shoulders sprang back again, and banged him on the flank, and great trails of creepers, all matted together, hung from his tusks as he threw his head from side to side and ploughed out his pathway. Then Little Toomai laid himself down close to the great neck, lest a swinging bough should sweep him to the ground, and he wished that he were back in the lines again.

The grass began to get squashy, and Kala Nag's feet sucked and squelched as he put them down, and the night mist at the bottom of the valley chilled Little Toomai. There was a splash and a trample, and the rush of running water, and Kala Nag strode through the bed of a river, feeling his way at each step. Above the noise of the water, as it swirled round the elephant's legs, Little Toomai could hear more splashing and some trumpeting both up stream and down—great grunts and angry snortings, and all the mist about him seemed to be full of rolling, wavy shadows.

"*Ai!*" he said, half aloud, his teeth chattering. "The elephant-folk are out to-night. It *is* the dance, then."

Kala Nag swashed out of the water, blew his trunk clear, and began another climb; but this time he was not alone, and he had not to make his path. That was made already, six feet wide, in front of him, where the bent jungle-grass was trying to recover itself and stand up. Many elephants must have gone that way only a few minutes before. Little Toomai looked back, and behind him a great wild tusker, with his little pig's eyes glowing like hot coals, was just lifting himself out of the misty river. Then the trees closed up again, and they went on and up, with trumpetings and crashings, and the sound of breaking branches on every side of them.

At last Kala Nag stood still between two tree-

trunks at the very top of the hill. They were part of a circle of trees that grew round an irregular space of some three or four acres, and in all that space, as Little Toomai could see, the ground had been trampled down as hard as a brick floor. Some trees grew in the centre of the clearing, but their bark was rubbed away, and the white wood beneath showed all shiny and polished in the patches of moonlight. There were creepers hanging from the upper branches, and the bells of the flowers of the creepers, great waxy white things like convolvuluses, hung down fast asleep; but within the limits of the clearing there was not a single blade of green—nothing but the trampled earth.

The moonlight showed it all iron-gray, except where some elephants stood upon it, and their shadows were inky black. Little Toomai looked, holding his breath, with his eyes starting out of his head, and as he looked, more and more and more elephants swung out into the open from between the tree-trunks. Little Toomai could count only up to ten, and he counted again and again on his fingers till he lost count of the tens, and his head began to swim. Outside the clearing he could hear them crashing in the undergrowth as they worked their way up the hillside; but as soon as they were within the circle of the tree-trunks they moved like ghosts.

There were white-tusked wild males, with fallen leaves and nuts and twigs lying in the wrinkles of their necks and the folds of their ears; fat, slow-footed she-elephants, with restless little pinky-black calves only three or four feet high running under their stomachs; young elephants with their tusks just beginning to show, and very proud of them; lanky, scraggy old-maid elephants, with their hollow, anxious faces, and trunks like rough bark; savage old bull-elephants, scarred from shoulder to flank with great weals and cuts of bygone fights, and the caked dirt of their solitary mud-baths dropping from their shoulders; and there was one with a broken tusk and the marks of the full-stroke, the terrible drawing scrape, of a tiger's claws on his side.

They were standing head to head, or walking to and fro across the ground in couples, or rocking and swaying all by themselves—scores and scores of elephants.

Toomai knew that, so long as he lay still on Kala Nag's neck, nothing would happen to him; for even in the rush and scramble of a Keddah-drive a wild elephant does not reach up with his trunk and drag a man off the neck of a tame elephant; and these elephants were not thinking of men that night. Once they started and put their ears forward when they heard the chinking of a leg-iron in the forest, but it was Pudmini, Petersen Sahib's pet elephant, her chain snapped short off, grunting, snuffling up the hillside. She must have broken her pickets, and come straight from Petersen Sahib's camp; and Little Toomai saw another elephant, one that he did not know, with deep rope-galls on his back and breast. He, too, must have run away from some camp in the hills about.

At last there was no sound of any more elephants moving in the forest, and Kala Nag rolled out from his station between the trees and went into the middle of the crowd, clucking and gurgling, and all the elephants began to talk in their own tongue, and to move about.

Still lying down, Little Toomai looked down upon scores and scores of broad backs, and wagging ears, and tossing trunks, and little rolling eyes. He heard the click of tusks as they crossed other tusks by accident, and the dry rustle of trunks twined together, and the chafing of enormous sides and shoulders in the crowd, and the incessant flick and *hissh* of the great tails. Then a cloud came over the moon, and he sat in black darkness; but the quiet, steady hustling and pushing and gurgling went on just the same. He knew that there were elephants all round Kala Nag, and that there was no chance of backing him out of the assembly; so he set his teeth and shivered. In a Keddah at least there was torch-light and shouting, but here he was all alone in the dark, and once a trunk came up and touched him on the knee.

Then an elephant trumpeted, and they all took it up for five or ten terrible seconds. The dew from the trees above spattered down like rain on the unseen backs, and a dull booming noise began, not very loud at first, and Little Toomai could not tell what it was; but it grew and grew, and Kala Nag lifted up one fore foot and then the other, and brought them down on the ground—one-two, one-two, as steadily as trip-hammers. The elephants were stamping all together now, and it sounded like a war-drum beaten at the mouth of a cave. The dew fell from the trees till there was no more left to fall, and the booming went on, and the ground rocked and shivered, and Little Toomai put his hands up to his ears to shut out the sound. But it was all one gigantic jar that ran through him—this stamp of hundreds of heavy feet on the raw earth. Once or twice he could feel Kala Nag and all the others surge forward a few strides, and the thumping would change to the crushing sound of juicy green things being bruised, but in a minute or two the boom of feet on hard earth began again. A tree was creaking and groaning somewhere near him. He put out his arm and felt the bark, but Kala Nag moved forward, still tramping, and he could not tell where he was in the clearing. There was no sound from the elephants, except once, when two or three little calves squeaked together. Then he heard a thump and a shuffle, and the booming went on. It must have lasted fully two hours, and Little Toomai ached in every nerve; but he knew by the smell of the night air that the dawn was coming.

The morning broke in one sheet of pale yellow behind the green hills, and the booming stopped with the first ray, as though the light had been an order. Before Little Toomai had got the ringing out of his head, before even he had shifted his position, there was not an elephant in sight except Kala Nag, Pudmini, and the elephant with the rope-galls, and there was neither sign nor rustle nor whisper down the hillsides to show where the others had gone.

Little Toomai stared again and again. The clearing, as he remembered it, had grown in the night. More trees stood in the middle of it, but the undergrowth and the jungle-grass at the sides had been rolled back. Little Toomai stared once more. Now he understood the trampling. The elephants had stamped out more room—had stamped the thick grass and juicy cane to trash, the trash into slivers, the slivers into tiny fibres, and the fibres into hard earth.

"Wah!" said Little Toomai, and his eyes were very heavy. "Kala Nag, my lord, let us keep by Pudmini and go to Petersen Sahib's camp, or I shall drop from thy neck."

The third elephant watched the two go away, snorted, wheeled round, and took his own path. He may have belonged to some little native king's establishment, fifty or sixty or a hundred miles away.

Two hours later, as Petersen Sahib was eating early breakfast, the elephants, who had been double-chained that night, began to trumpet, and Pudmini, mired to the shoulders, with Kala Nag, very foot-sore, shambled into the camp.

Little Toomai's face was gray and pinched, and his hair was full of leaves and drenched with dew; but he tried to salute Petersen Sahib, and cried faintly: "The dance—the elephant-dance! I have seen it, and—I die!" As Kala Nag sat down, he slid off his neck in a dead faint.

But, since native children have no nerves worth speaking of, in two hours he was lying very contentedly in Petersen Sahib's hammock with Petersen Sahib's shooting-coat under his head, and a glass of warm milk, a little brandy, with a dash of quinine inside of him; and while the old hairy, scarred hunters of the jungles sat three-deep before him, looking at him as though he were a spirit, he told his tale in short words, as a child will, and wound up with:

"Now, if I lie in one word, send men to see, and they will find that the elephant-folk have trampled down more room in their dance-room, and they will find ten and ten, and many times ten, tracks leading to that dance-room. They made more room with their feet. I have seen it. Kala Nag took me, and I saw. Also Kala Nag is very leg-weary!"

Little Toomai lay back and slept all through the long afternoon and into the twilight, and while he

slept Petersen Sahib and Machua Appa followed the
track of the two elephants for fifteen miles across the
hills. Petersen Sahib had spent eighteen years in catching elephants, and he had only once before found such
a dance-place. Machua Appa had no need to look
twice at the clearing to see what had been done there,
or to scratch with his toe in the packed, rammed earth.

"The child speaks truth," said he. "All this was done
last night, and I have counted seventy tracks crossing
the river. See, Sahib, where Pudmini's leg-iron cut the
bark off that tree! Yes; she was there too."

They looked at each other, and up and down, and
they wondered; for the ways of elephants are beyond
the wit of any man, black or white, to fathom.

"Forty years and five," said Machua Appa, "have I
followed my lord, the elephant, but never have I heard
that any child of man had seen what this child has
seen. By all the Gods of the Hills, it is—what can we
say?" and he shook his head.

When they got back to camp it was time for the
evening meal. Petersen Sahib ate alone in his tent, but
he gave orders that the camp should have two sheep
and some fowls, as well as a double ration of flour and
rice and salt, for he knew that there would be a feast.

Big Toomai had come up hot-foot from the camp
in the plains to search for his son and his elephant, and
now that he had found them he looked at them as
though he were afraid of them both. And there was a
feast by the blazing camp-fires in front of the lines of
picketed elephants, and Little Toomai was the hero of
it all; and the big brown elephant-catchers, the trackers
and drivers and ropers, and the men who know all the
secrets of breaking the wildest elephants, passed him
from one to the other, and they marked his forehead
with blood from the breast of a newly killed jungle-

cock, to show that he was a forester, initiated and free of all the jungles.

And at last, when the flames died down, and the red light of the logs made the elephants look as though they had been dipped in blood too, Machua Appa, the head of all the drivers of all the Keddahs,—Machua Appa, Petersen Sahib's otherself, who had never seen a made road in forty years: Machua Appa, who was so great that he had no other name than Machua Appa, —leaped to his feet, with Little Toomai held high in the air above his head, and shouted: "Listen, my brothers. Listen, too, you my lords in the lines there, for I, Machua Appa, am speaking! This little one shall no more be called Little Toomai, but Toomai of the Elephants, as his great-grandfather was called before him. What never man has seen he has seen through the long night, and the favour of the elephant-folk and of the Gods of the Jungles is with him. He shall become a great tracker; he shall become greater than I, even I—Machua Appa! He shall follow the new trail, and the stale trail, and the mixed trail, with a clear eye! He shall take no harm in the Keddah when he runs under their bellies to rope the wild tuskers; and if he slips before the feet of the charging bull-elephant, that bull-elephant shall know who he is and shall not crush him. *Aihai!* my lords in the chains,"—he whirled up the line of pickets,—"here is the little one that has seen your dances in your hidden places—the sight that never man saw! Give him honour, my lords! *Salaam karo*, my children. Make your salute to Toomai of the Elephants! Gunga Pershad, ahaa! Hira Guj, Birchi Guj, Kuttar Guj, ahaa! Pudmini,—thou hast seen him at the dance, and thou too, Kala Nag, my pearl among elephants!—ahaa! Together! To Toomai of the Elephants. *Barrao!*"

And at that last wild yell the whole line flung up their trunks till the tips touched their foreheads, and broke out into the full salute, the crashing trumpet-peal that only the Viceroy of India hears—the Salaamut of the Keddah.

But it was all for the sake of Little Toomai, who had seen what never man had seen before—the dance of the elephants at night and alone in the heart of the Garo hills!

SHIV AND THE GRASSHOPPER

(The Song that Toomai's Mother sang to the Baby)

*Shiv, who poured the harvest and made the winds to
  blow,*
Sitting at the doorways of a day of long ago,
Gave to each his portion, food and toil and fate,
*From the King upon the guddee to the Beggar at the
  gate.*
   All things made he—Shiva the Preserver.
   Mahadeo! Mahadeo! He made all,—
   Thorn for the camel, fodder for the kine,
   And mother's heart for sleepy head, O little son of
   mine!

Wheat he gave to rich folk, millet to the poor,
*Broken scraps for holy men that beg from door to
  door;*
Cattle to the tiger, carrion to the kite,
*And rags and bones to wicked wolves without the
  wall at night.*
Naught he found too lofty, none he saw too low—
Parbati beside him watched them come and go;
Thought to cheat her husband, turning Shiv to jest—
Stole the little grasshopper and hid it in her breast.

So she tricked him, Shiva the Preserver.
Mahadeo! Mahadeo! turn and see.
Tall are the camels, heavy are the kine,
But this was least of little things, O little son of
  mine!

When the dole was ended, laughingly she said,
"Master, of a million mouths is not one unfed?"
Laughing, Shiv made answer, "All have had their part,
Even he, the little one, hidden next thy heart."
From her breast she plucked it, Parbati the thief,
Saw the Least of Little Things gnawed a new-grown
  leaf!
Saw and feared and wondered, making prayer to Shiv,
Who hath surely given meat to all that live.

All things made he—Shiva the Preserver.
Mahadeo! Mahadeo! He made all,—
Thorn for the camel, fodder for the kine,
And mother's heart for sleepy head, O little son of
  mine!

". . . TO HAUL AND PILE BIG BAULKS OF TEAK IN THE TIMBER-YARDS
AT MOULMEIN" (*page 148*)

HER MAJESTY'S
SERVANTS

HER MAJESTY'S SERVANTS

You can work it out by Fractions or by simple Rule
 of Three,
But the way of Tweedle-dum is not the way of
 Tweedle-dee.
You can twist it, you can turn it, you can plait it till
 you drop,
But the way of Pilly-Winky's not the way of Winkie-
 Pop!

IT HAD been raining heavily for one whole month
—raining on a camp of thirty thousand men, thousands
of camels, elephants, horses, bullocks, and mules, all
gathered together at a place called Rawal Pindi, to be
reviewed by the Viceroy of India. He was receiving a
visit from the Amir of Afghanistan—a wild king of
a very wild country; and the Amir had brought with
him for a bodyguard eight hundred men and horses
who had never seen a camp or a locomotive before in
their lives—savage men and savage horses from somewhere at the back of Central Asia. Every night a mob
of these horses would be sure to break their heel-ropes,
and stampede up and down the camp through the mud
in the dark, or the camels would break loose and run
about and fall over the ropes of the tents, and you can

imagine how pleasant that was for men trying to go to sleep. My tent lay far away from the camel lines, and I thought it was safe; but one night a man popped his head in and shouted, "Get out, quick! They're coming! My tent's gone!"

I knew who "they" were; so I put on my boots and waterproof and scuttled out into the slush. Little Vixen, my fox-terrier, went out through the other side; and then there was a roaring and a grunting and bubbling, and I saw the tent cave in, as the pole snapped, and begin to dance about like a mad ghost. A camel had blundered into it, and wet and angry as I was, I could not help laughing. Then I ran on, because I did not know how many camels might have got loose, and before long I was out of sight of the camp, ploughing my way through the mud.

At last I fell over the tail-end of a gun, and by that knew I was somewhere near the Artillery lines where the cannon were stacked at night. As I did not want to plowter about any more in the drizzle and the dark, I put my waterproof over the muzzle of one gun, and made a sort of wigwam with two or three rammers that I found, and lay along the tail of another gun, wondering where Vixen had got to, and where I might be.

Just as I was getting ready to sleep I heard a jingle of harness and a grunt, and a mule passed me shaking his wet ears. He belonged to a screw-gun battery, for I could hear the rattle of the straps and rings and chains and things on his saddle-pad. The screw-guns are tiny little cannon made in two pieces that are screwed together when the time comes to use them. They are taken up mountains, anywhere that a mule can find a road, and they are very useful for fighting in rocky country.

Behind the mule there was a camel, with his big soft feet squelching and slipping in the mud, and his neck bobbing to and fro like a strayed hen's. Luckily, I knew enough of beast language—not wild-beast language, but camp-beast language, of course—from the natives to know what he was saying.

He must have been the one that flopped into my tent, for he called to the mule, "What shall I do? Where shall I go? I have fought with a white thing that waved, and it took a stick and hit me on the neck." (That was my broken tent-pole, and I was very glad to know it.) "Shall we run on?"

"Oh, it was you," said the mule, "you and your friends, that have been disturbing the camp? All right. You'll be beaten for this in the morning; but I may as well give you something on account now."

I heard the harness jingle as the mule backed and caught the camel two kicks in the ribs that rang like a drum. "Another time," he said, "you'll know better than to run through a mule-battery at night, shouting 'Thieves and fire!' Sit down, and keep your silly neck quiet."

The camel doubled up camel-fashion, like a two-foot rule, and sat down whimpering. There was a regular beat of hoofs in the darkness, and a big troop-horse cantered up as steadily as though he were on parade, jumped a gun-tail, and landed close to the mule.

"It's disgraceful," he said, blowing out his nostrils. "Those camels have racketed through our lines again —the third time this week. How's a horse to keep his condition if he isn't allowed to sleep. Who's here?"

"I'm the breech-piece mule of number two gun of the First Screw Battery," said the mule, "and the other's one of your friends. He's waked me up too. Who are you?"

"Number Fifteen, E troop, Ninth Lancers—Dick Cunliffe's horse. Stand over a little, there."

"Oh, beg your pardon," said the mule. "It's too dark to see much. Aren't these camels too sickening for anything? I walked out of my lines to get a little peace and quiet here."

"My lords," said the camel humbly, "we dreamed bad dreams in the night, and we were very much afraid. I am only a baggage-camel of the 39th Native Infantry, and I am not so brave as you are, my lords."

"Then why the pickets didn't you stay and carry baggage for the 39th Native Infantry, instead of running all round the camp?" said the mule.

"They were such very bad dreams," said the camel. "I am sorry. Listen! What is that? Shall we run on again?"

"Sit down," said the mule, "or you'll snap your long legs between the guns." He cocked one ear and listened. "Bullocks!" he said. "Gun-bullocks. On my word, you and your friends have waked the camp very thoroughly. It takes a good deal of prodding to put up a gun-bullock."

I heard a chain dragging along the ground, and a yoke of the great sulky white bullocks that drag the

heavy siege-guns when the elephants won't go any nearer to the firing, came shouldering along together; and almost stepping on the chain was another battery-mule, calling wildly for "Billy."

"That's one of our recruits," said the old mule to the troop-horse. "He's calling for me. Here, youngster, stop squealing. The dark never hurt anybody yet."

The gun-bullocks lay down together and began chewing the cud, but the young mule huddled close to Billy.

"Things!" he said. "Fearful and horrible things, Billy! They came into our lines while we were asleep. D'you think they'll kill us?"

"I've a very great mind to give you a number-one kicking," said Billy. "The idea of a fourteen-hand mule with your training disgracing the battery before this gentleman!"

"Gently, gently!" said the troop-horse. "Remember they are always like this to begin with. The first time I ever saw a man (it was in Australia when I was a three-year-old) I ran for half a day, and if I'd seen a camel I should have been running still."

Nearly all our horses for the English cavalry are brought to India from Australia, and are broken in by the troopers themselves.

"True enough," said Billy. "Stop shaking, youngster. The first time they put the full harness with all its chains on my back, I stood on my fore legs and kicked every bit of it off. I hadn't learned the real science of kicking then, but the battery said they had never seen anything like it."

"But this wasn't harness or anything that jingled," said the young mule. "You know I don't mind that now, Billy. It was Things like trees, and they fell up and down the lines and bubbled; and my head-rope broke, and I couldn't find my driver, and I couldn't find you, Billy, so I ran off with—with these gentlemen."

"H'm!" said Billy. "As soon as I heard the camels were loose I came away on my own account, quietly. When a battery—a screw-gun mule calls gun-bullocks gentlemen, he must be very badly shaken up. Who are you fellows on the ground there?"

The gun-bullocks rolled their cuds, and answered both together: "The seventh yoke of the first gun of the Big Gun Battery. We were asleep when the camels came, but when we were trampled on we got up and walked away. It is better to lie quiet in the mud than to be disturbed on good bedding. We told your friend here that there was nothing to be afraid of, but he knew so much that he thought otherwise. Wah!"

They went on chewing.

"That comes of being afraid," said Billy. "You get laughed at by gun-bullocks. I hope you like it, young un."

The young mule's teeth snapped, and I heard him say something about not being afraid of any beefy old bullock in the world; but the bullocks only clicked their horns together and went on chewing.

"Now, don't be angry *after* you've been afraid. That's the worst kind of cowardice," said the troop-horse. "Anybody can be forgiven for being scared in the night, *I* think, if they see things they don't understand. We've broken out of our pickets, again and again, four hundred and fifty of us, just because a new recruit got to telling tales of whip-snakes at home in Australia till we were scared to death of the loose ends of our head-ropes."

"That's all very well in camp," said Billy; "I'm not above stampeding myself, for the fun of the thing, when I haven't been out for a day or two; but what do you do on active service?"

"Oh, that's quite another set of new shoes," said the troop-horse. "Dick Cunliffe's on my back then, and drives his knees into me, and all I have to do is to watch where I am putting my feet, and to keep my hind legs well under me, and be bridle-wise."

"What's bridle-wise?" said the young mule.

"By the Blue Gums of the Back Blocks," snorted the troop-horse, "do you mean to say that you aren't taught to be bridle-wise in your business? How can you do anything, unless you can spin round at once when the rein is pressed on your neck? It means life or death to your man, and of course that's life or death to you. Get round with your hind legs under you the instant you feel the rein on your neck. If you haven't room to swing round, rear up a little and come round on your hind legs. That's being bridle-wise."

"We aren't taught that way," said Billy the mule stiffly. "We're taught to obey the man at our head: step off when he says so, and step in when he says so. I suppose it comes to the same thing. Now, with all this fine fancy business and rearing, which must be very bad for your hocks, what do you *do?*"

"That depends," said the troop-horse. "Generally I have to go in among a lot of yelling, hairy men with knives,—long shiny knives, worse than the farrier's knives,—and I have to take care that Dick's boot is just touching the next man's boot without crushing it. I can see Dick's lance to the right of my right eye, and I know I'm safe. I shouldn't care to be the man or horse that stood up to Dick and me when we're in a hurry."

"Don't the knives hurt?" said the young mule.

"Well, I got one cut across the chest once, but that wasn't Dick's fault——"

"A lot I should have cared whose fault it was, if it hurt!" said the young mule.

"You must," said the troop-horse. "If you don't trust your man, you may as well run away at once. That's what some of our horses do, and I don't blame them. As I was saying, it wasn't Dick's fault. The man was lying on the ground, and I stretched myself not to tread on him, and he slashed up at me. Next time I have to go over a man lying down I shall step on him—hard."

"H'm!" said Billy; "it sounds very foolish. Knives are dirty things at any time. The proper thing to do is to climb up a mountain with a well-balanced saddle, hang on by all four feet and your ears too, and creep and crawl and wriggle along, till you come out hundreds of feet above any one else, on a ledge where there's just room enough for your hoofs. Then you stand still and keep quiet,—never ask a man to hold your head, young un,—keep quiet while the guns are being put together, and then you watch the little poppy shells drop down into the tree-tops ever so far below."

"Don't you ever trip?" said the troop-horse.

"They say that when a mule trips you can split a hen's ear," said Billy. "Now and again *per-haps* a badly-packed saddle will upset a mule, but it's very seldom. I wish I could show you our business. It's beautiful. Why, it took me three years to find out what the men were driving at. The science of the thing is never to show up against the sky-line, because, if you do, you may get fired at. Remember that, young un. Always keep hidden as much as possible, even if you have to go a mile out of your way. I lead the battery when it comes to that sort of climbing."

"Fired at without the chance of running into the people who are firing!" said the troop-horse, thinking hard. "I couldn't stand that. I should want to charge, with Dick."

"Oh no, you wouldn't; you know that as soon as the guns are in position *they'll* do all the charging. That's scientific and neat; but knives—pah!"

The baggage-camel had been bobbing his head to and fro for some time past, anxious to get a word in edgeways. Then I heard him say, as he cleared his throat, nervously:

"I—I—I have fought a little, but not in that climbing way or that running way."

"No. Now you mention it," said Billy, "you don't look as though you were made for climbing or running —much. Well, how was it, old Haybales?"

"The proper way," said the camel. "We all sat down——"

"Oh, my crupper and breastplate!" said the troop-horse under his breath. "Sat down?"

"We sat down—a hundred of us," the camel went on, "in a big square, and the men piled our packs and saddles outside the square, and they fired over our backs, the men did, on all sides of the square."

"What sort of men? Any men that came along?" said the troop-horse. "They teach us in riding-school to lie down and let our masters fire across us, but Dick Cunliffe is the only man I'd trust to do that. It tickles my girths, and, besides, I can't see with my head on the ground."

"What does it matter who fires across you?" said the camel. "There are plenty of men and plenty of other camels close by, and a great many clouds of smoke. I am not frightened then. I sit still and wait."

"And yet," said Billy, "you dream bad dreams and upset the camp at night. Well! well! Before I'd lie down, not to speak of sitting down, and let a man fire across me, my heels and his head would have something to say to each other. Did you ever hear anything so awful as that?"

There was a long silence, and then one of the gun-bullocks lifted up his big head and said, "This is very foolish indeed. There is only one way of fighting."

"Oh, go on," said Billy. "*Please* don't mind me. I suppose you fellows fight standing on your tails?"

"Only one way," said the two together. (They must have been twins.) "This is the way. To put all twenty yoke of us to the big gun as soon as Two Tails trumpets." ("Two Tails" is camp slang for the elephant.)

"What does Two Tails trumpet for?" said the young mule.

"To show that he is not going any nearer to the smoke on the other side. Two Tails is a great coward. Then we tug the big gun all together—*Heya—Hullah! Heeyah! Hullah! We* do not climb like cats nor run like calves. We go across the level plain, twenty yoke of us, till we are unyoked again, and we graze while the big guns talk across the plain to some town with mud walls, and pieces of the wall fall out, and the dust goes up as though many cattle were coming home."

"Oh! And you choose that time for grazing, do you?" said the young mule.

"That time or any other. Eating is always good. We wait till we are yoked up again and tug the gun back to where Two Tails is waiting for it. Sometimes there are big guns in the city that speak back, and some of us are killed, and then there is all the more grazing for those that are left. This is Fate—nothing but Fate. None the less, Two Tails is a great coward. That is the proper way to fight. We are brothers from Hapur.

Our father was a sacred bull of Shiva. We have spoken."

"Well, I've certainly learned something to-night," said the troop-horse. "Do you gentlemen of the screw-gun battery feel inclined to eat when you are being fired at with big guns, and Two Tails is behind you?"

"About as much as we feel inclined to sit down and let men sprawl all over us, or run into people with knives. I never heard such stuff. A mountain ledge, a well-balanced load, a driver you can trust to let you pick your own way, and I'm your mule; but the other things—no!" said Billy, with a stamp of his foot.

"Of course," said the troop-horse, "every one is not made in the same way, and I can quite see that your family, on your father's side, would fail to understand a great many things."

"Never you mind my family on my father's side," said Billy angrily, for every mule hates to be reminded that his father was a donkey. "My father was a Southern gentleman, and he could pull down and bite and kick into rags every horse he came across. Remember that, you big brown Brumby!"

Brumby means wild horse without any breeding. Imagine the feelings of Sunol if a car-horse called her a "skate," and you can imagine how the Australian horse felt. I saw the white of his eye glitter in the dark.

"See here, you son of an imported Malaga jackass," he said between his teeth, "I'd have you know that I'm related on my mother's side to Carbine, winner of the Melbourne Cup; and where *I* come from we aren't accustomed to being ridden over roughshod by any parrot-mouthed, pig-headed mule in a pop-gun pea-shooter battery. Are you ready?"

"On your hind legs!" squealed Billy. They both

reared up facing each other, and I was expecting a furious fight, when a gurgly, rumbly voice called out of the darkness to the right: "Children, what are you fighting about there? Be quiet."

Both beasts dropped down with a snort of disgust, for neither horse nor mule can bear to listen to an elephant's voice.

"It's Two Tails!" said the troop-horse. "I can't stand him. A tail at each end isn't fair!"

"My feelings exactly," said Billy, crowding into the troop-horse for company. "We're very alike in some things."

"I suppose we've inherited them from our mothers," said the troop-horse. "It's not worth quarrelling about. Hi! Two Tails, are you tied up?"

"Yes," said Two Tails, with a laugh all up his trunk. "I'm picketed for the night. I've heard what you fellows have been saying. But don't be afraid. I'm not coming over."

The bullocks and the camel said, half aloud: "Afraid of Two Tails—what nonsense!" And the bullocks went on: "We are sorry that you heard, but it is true. Two Tails, why are you afraid of the guns when they fire?"

"Well," said Two Tails, rubbing one hind leg against the other, exactly like a little boy saying poetry, "I don't quite know whether you'd understand."

"We don't, but we have to pull the guns," said the bullocks.

"I know it, and I know you are a good deal braver than you think you are. But it's different with me. My battery captain called me a Pachydermatous Anachronism the other day."

"That's another way of fighting, I suppose?" said Billy, who was recovering his spirits.

"*You* don't know what that means, of course, but I

do. It means betwixt and between, and that is just where I am. I can see inside my head what will happen when a shell bursts; and you bullocks can't."

"I can," said the troop-horse. "At least a little bit. I try not to think about it."

"I can see more than you, and I *do* think about it. I know there's a great deal of me to take care of, and I know that nobody knows how to cure me when I'm sick. All they can do is to stop my driver's pay till I get well, and I can't trust my driver."

"Ah!" said the troop-horse. "That explains it. I can trust Dick."

"You could put a whole regiment of Dicks on my back without making me feel any better. I know just enough to be uncomfortable, and not enough to go on in spite of it."

"We do not understand," said the bullocks.

"I know you don't. I'm not talking to you. You don't know what blood is."

"We do," said the bullocks. "It is red stuff that soaks into the ground and smells."

The troop-horse gave a kick and a bound and a snort.

"Don't talk of it," he said. "I can smell it now, just thinking of it. It makes me want to run—when I haven't Dick on my back."

"But it is not here," said the camel and the bullocks. "Why are you so stupid?"

"It's vile stuff," said Billy. "I don't want to run, but I don't want to talk about it."

"There you are!" said Two Tails, waving his tail to explain.

"Surely. Yes, we have been here all night," said the bullocks.

Two Tails stamped his foot till the iron ring on it

jingled. "Oh, I'm not talking to *you*. You can't see inside your heads."

"No. We see out of our four eyes," said the bullocks. "We see straight in front of us."

"If I could do that and nothing else you wouldn't be needed to pull the big guns at all. If I was like my captain—he can see things inside his head before the firing begins, and he shakes all over, but he knows too much to run away—if I was like him I could pull the guns. But if I were as wise as all that I should never be here. I should be a king in the forest, as I used to be, sleeping half the day and bathing when I liked. I haven't had a good bath for a month."

"That's all very fine," said Billy; "but giving a thing a long name doesn't make it any better."

"H'sh!" said the troop-horse. "I think I understand what Two Tails means."

"You'll understand better in a minute," said Two Tails angrily. "Now, just you explain to me why you don't like *this!*"

He began trumpeting furiously at the top of his trumpet.

"Stop that!" said Billy and the troop-horse together, and I could hear them stamp and shiver. An elephant's trumpeting is always nasty, especially on a dark night.

"I shan't stop," said Two Tails. "Won't you explain that, please? *Hhrrmph! Rrrt! Rrrmph! Rrrhha!*" Then he stopped suddenly, and I heard a little whimper in the dark, and knew that Vixen had found me at last. She knew as well as I did that if there is one thing in the world the elephant is more afraid of than another, it is a little barking dog; so she stopped to bully Two Tails in his pickets, and yapped round his big feet. Two Tails shuffled and squeaked. "Go away, little dog!" he said. "Don't snuff at my ankles, or I'll kick at

you. Good little dog—nice little doggie, then! Go
home, you yelping little beast! Oh, why doesn't some
one take her away? She'll bite me in a minute."

"Seems to me," said Billy to the troop-horse, "that
our friend Two Tails is afraid of most things. Now, if
I had a full meal for every dog I've kicked across the
parade-ground, I should be nearly as fat as Two Tails."

I whistled, and Vixen ran up to me, muddy all over,
and licked my nose, and told me a long tale about hunting for me all through the camp. I never let her know
that I understood beast talk, or she would have taken
all sorts of liberties. So I buttoned her into the breast
of my overcoat, and Two Tails shuffled and stamped
and growled to himself.

"Extraordinary! Most extraordinary!" he said. "It
runs in our family. Now, where has that nasty little
beast gone to?"

I heard him feeling about with his trunk.

"We all seem to be affected in various ways," he
went on, blowing his nose. "Now, you gentlemen were
alarmed, I believe, when I trumpeted."

"Not alarmed, exactly," said the troop-horse, "but
it made me feel as though I had hornets where my
saddle ought to be. Don't begin again."

"I'm frightened of a little dog, and the camel here
is frightened by bad dreams in the night."

"It is very lucky for us that we haven't all got to
fight in the same way," said the troop-horse.

"What I want to know," said the young mule, who
had been quiet for a long while—"what *I* want to know
is, why we have to fight at all."

"Because we're told to," said the troop-horse, with
a snort of contempt.

"Orders," said Billy the mule; and his teeth snapped.

"*Hukm hai!*" (It is an order), said the camel with

a gurgle; and Two Tails and the bullocks repeated, *"Hukm hai!"*

"Yes, but who gives the orders?" said the recruit-mule.

"The man who walks at your head—Or sits on your back—Or holds your nose-rope—Or twists your tail," said Billy and the troop-horse and the camel and the bullocks one after the other.

"But who gives them the orders?"

"Now you want to know too much, young un," said Billy, "and that is one way of getting kicked. All you have to do is to obey the man at your head and ask no questions."

"He's quite right," said Two Tails. "I can't always obey, because I'm betwixt and between; but Billy's right. Obey the man next to you who gives the order, or you'll stop all the battery, besides getting a thrashing."

The gun-bullocks got up to go. "Morning is coming," they said. "We will go back to our lines. It is true that we see only out of our eyes, and we are not very clever; but still, we are the only people to-night who have not been afraid. Good-night, you brave people."

Nobody answered, and the troop-horse said, to change the conversation, "Where's that little dog? A dog means a man somewhere about."

"Here I am," yapped Vixen, "under the gun-tail with my man. You big, blundering beast of a camel you, you upset our tent. My man's very angry."

"Phew!" said the bullocks. "He must be white?"

"Of course he is," said Vixen. "Do you suppose I'm looked after by a black bullock-driver?"

"Huah! Ouach! Ugh!" said the bullocks. "Let us get away quickly."

They plunged forward in the mud, and managed

somehow to run their yoke on the pole of an ammuni-tion-waggon, where it jammed.

"Now you *have* done it," said Billy calmly. "Don't struggle. You're hung up till daylight. What on earth's the matter?"

The bullocks went off into the long, hissing snorts that Indian cattle give, and pushed and crowded and slued and stamped and slipped and nearly fell down in the mud, grunting savagely.

"You'll break your necks in a minute," said the troop-horse. "What's the matter with white men? I live with 'em."

"They—eat—us! Pull!" said the near bullock: the yoke snapped with a twang, and they lumbered off together.

I never knew before what made Indian cattle so scared of Englishmen. We eat beef—a thing that no cattle-driver touches—and of course the cattle do not like it.

"May I be flogged with my own pad-chains! Who'd have thought of two big lumps like those losing their heads?" said Billy.

"Never mind. I'm going to look at this man. Most of the white men, I know, have things in their pockets," said the troop-horse.

"I'll leave you then. I can't say I'm over-fond of 'em myself. Besides, white men who haven't a place to sleep in are more than likely to be thieves, and I've a good deal of Government property on my back. Come along, young un, and we'll go back to our lines. Good-night, Australia! 'See you on parade to-morrow, I suppose. Good-night, old Hay-bale!—try to control your feel-ings, won't you? Good-night, Two Tails! If you pass us on the ground to-morrow, don't trumpet. It spoils our formation."

Billy the mule stumped off with the swaggering limp

of an old campaigner, as the troop-horse's head came nuzzling into my breast, and I gave him biscuits; while Vixen, who is a most conceited little dog, told him fibs about the scores of horses that she and I kept.

"I'm coming to the parade to-morrow in my dog-cart," she said. "Where will you be?"

"On the left hand of the second squadron. I set the time for all my troop, little lady," he said politely. "Now I must go back to Dick. My tail's all muddy, and he'll have two hours' hard work dressing me for parade."

The big parade of all the thirty thousand men was held that afternoon, and Vixen and I had a good place close to the Viceroy and the Amir of Afghanistan, with his high, big black hat of astrakhan wool and the great diamond star in the centre. The first part of the review was all sunshine, and the regiments went by in wave upon wave of legs all moving together, and guns all in a line, till our eyes grew dizzy. Then the cavalry came up, to the beautiful cavalry canter of "Bonnie Dundee," and Vixen cocked her ear where she sat on the dog-cart. The second squadron of the Lancers shot by, and there was the troop-horse, with his tail like spun silk, his head pulled into his breast, one ear forward and one back, setting the time for all his squadron, his legs going as smoothly as waltz-music. Then the big guns came by, and I saw Two Tails and two other elephants harnessed in line to a forty-pounder siege-gun, while twenty yoke of oxen walked behind. The seventh pair had a new yoke, and they looked rather stiff and tired. Last came the screw-guns, and Billy the mule carried himself as though he commanded all the troops, and his harness was oiled and polished till it winked. I gave a cheer all by myself for Billy the mule, but he never looked right or left.

The rain began to fall again, and for a while it was too misty to see what the troops were doing. They had made a big half-circle across the plain, and were spreading out into a line. That line grew and grew and grew till it was three-quarters of a mile long from wing to wing—one solid wall of men, horses, and guns. Then it came on straight toward the Viceroy and the Amir, and as it got nearer the ground began to shake, like the deck of a steamer when the engines are going fast.

Unless you have been there you cannot imagine what a frightening effect this steady come down of troops has on the spectators, even when they know it is only a review. I looked at the Amir. Up till then he had not shown the shadow of a sign of astonishment or anything else; but now his eyes began to get bigger and bigger, and he picked up the reins on his horse's neck and looked behind him. For a minute it seemed as though he were going to draw his sword and slash his way out through the English men and women in the carriages at the back. Then the advance stopped dead, the ground stood still, the whole line saluted, and thirty bands began to play all together. That was the end of the review, and the regiments went off to their camps in the rain; and an infantry band struck up—

> *The animals went in two by two,*
> *Hurrah!*
> *The animals went in two by two,*
> *The elephant and the battery mu-*
> *l', and they all got into the Ark*
> *For to get out of the rain!*

Then I heard an old grizzled, long-haired Central Asian chief, who had come down with the Amir, asking questions of a native officer.

"Now," said he, "in what manner was this wonderful thing done?"

And the officer answered, "There was an order, and they obeyed."

"But are the beasts as wise as the men?" said the chief.

"They obey, as the men do. Mule, horse, elephant, or bullock, he obeys his driver, and the driver his sergeant, and the sergeant his lieutenant, and the lieutenant his captain, and the captain his major, and the major his colonel, and the colonel his brigadier commanding three regiments, and the brigadier his general, who obeys the Viceroy, who is the servant of the Empress. Thus it is done."

"Would it were so in Afghanistan!" said the chief; "for there we obey only our own wills."

"And for that reason," said the native officer, twirling his moustache, "your Amir whom you do not obey must come here and take orders from our Viceroy."

"IT HAD BEEN RAINING HEAVILY FOR ONE WHOLE MONTH . . ." (*page 177*)

PARADE-SONG OF THE CAMP-ANIMALS

ELEPHANTS OF THE GUN-TEAMS

We lent to Alexander the strength of Hercules,
The wisdom of our foreheads, the cunning of our
    knees.
We bowed our necks to service; they ne'er were
    loosed again,—
Make way there, way for the ten-foot teams
      Of the Forty-Pounder train!

GUN-BULLOCKS

Those heroes in their harnesses avoid a cannon-ball,
And what they know of powder upsets them one and
    all;
Then we come into action and tug the guns again,—
Make way there, way for the twenty yoke
      Of the Forty-Pounder train!

CAVALRY HORSES

By the brand on my withers, the finest of tunes
Is played by the Lancers, Hussars, and Dragoons,
And it's sweeter than "Stables" or "Water" to me,
The Cavalry Canter of "Bonnie Dundee"!

Then feed us and break us and handle and groom,
And give us good riders and plenty of room,
And launch us in column of squadron and see
The way of the war-horse to "Bonnie Dundee"!

SCREW-GUN MULES

As me and my companions were scrambling up a hill,
The path was lost in rolling stones, but we went
    forward still;
For we can wriggle and climb, my lads, and turn up
    everywhere,
And it's our delight on a mountain height, with a leg or
    two to spare!

Good luck to every sergeant, then, that lets us pick
    our road!
Bad luck to all the driver-men that cannot pack a load!
For we can wriggle and climb, my lads, and turn up
    everywhere,
And it's our delight on a mountain height, with a leg
    or two to spare!

COMMISSARIAT CAMELS

We haven't a camelty tune of our own
To help us trollop along,
But every neck is a hair-trombone
(Rtt-ta-ta-ta! is a hair-trombone!)
And this is our marching-song:
Can't! Don't! Shan't! Won't!
Pass it along the line!
Somebody's pack has slid from his back,
'Wish it were only mine!
Somebody's load has tipped off in the road—
Cheer for a halt and a row!
Urrr! Yarrh! Grr! Arrh!
Somebody's catching it now!

ALL THE BEASTS TOGETHER

Children of the Camp are we,
Serving each in his degree;
Children of the yoke and goad,
Pack and harness, pad and load.
See our line across the plain,
Like a heel-rope bent again,
Reaching, writhing, rolling far,
Sweeping all away to war!
While the men that walk beside,
Dusty, silent, heavy-eyed,
Cannot tell why we or they
March and suffer day by day.

    Children of the Camp are we,
    Serving each in his degree;
    Children of the yoke and goad,
    Pack and harness, pad and load.